The Hartwell Chronicles

Teenage Exorcist

Jen Lowry

The Hartwell Chronicles
Teenage Exorcist Series Book One by Jen Lowry

Cover Designer: The Magic Quill Graphics by Jessica Ozment

Thanks to Emmaline AH Mansfield for permission to print, Together We Stand Like Pine Trees In A Forest.
Public domain poetry, song lyrics, and Bible verses referenced

https://jenlowrywrites.com/   @jenlowrywrites
The Hartwell Chronicles Teenage Exorcist/Jen Lowry. – First Edition 2019
Library of Congress Control Number: 2019906969
Summary: Will Victoria and Tyler be able to save the world from demonic forces trying to burn it down? Can Victoria save her sister before it's too late?

ISBN for paperback version: ISBN: 978-1-7331381-0-9
{1. Horror Fiction 2. Supernatural Fiction 3. Paranormal Fiction 4. Clean Romance 5. Christianity 6. Faith 7. Demonic Possession 8. Exorcisms 9. Family Drama 10. Romance 11. Diverse

Typography by Monarch Educational Services, L.L.C.

7 6 5 4 3 2 1

Monarch Educational Services, L.L.C.
Clayton NC

The Hartwell Chronicles

Teenage Exorcist

Jen Lowry

Monarch Educational Services, L.L.C.
Clayton NC

Books by Jen Lowry

YA Fiction
The Hartwell Chronicles Teenage Exorcist Series
Bridges The Lightbearers Series (Monarch, 2019)
Sweet Potato Jones (Swoon Romance, 2020)

Dr. Jennifer Ikner Lowry
Challenge Devotional Series
Happy Renewal Year
Everyday Mom Challenge
30 Day Teacher Challenge
Fingerprint Curriculum

To Eli, for dreaming with me
To Solomon and Samuel, my loves forever

Modern Love: XXVII
George Meredith - 1828-1909

Distraction is the panacea, Sir!
I hear my oracle of Medicine say.
Doctor! that same specific yesterday
I tried, and the result will not deter
A second trial. Is the devil's line
Of golden hair, or raven black, composed?
And does a cheek, like any sea-shell rosed,
Or clear as widowed sky, seem most divine?
No matter, so I taste forgetfulness.
And if the devil snare me, body and mind,
Here gratefully I score:—he seemèd kind,
When not a soul would comfort my distress!
O sweet new world, in which I rise new made!
O Lady, once I gave love: now I take!
Lady, I must be flattered. Shouldst thou wake
The passion of a demon, be not afraid.

Let both grow together until the harvest: and in the time of harvest I will say to the reapers, Gather ye together first the tares, and bind them in bundles to burn them: but gather the wheat into my barn.

Matthew 13:30

Special Thanks

Grateful acknowledgment to the gifted Indigenous artist, Emmaline A.H. Mansfield, for permission to include original woodcut artwork (print 2/4), "Together We Stand Like Pine Trees in a Forest."

To view her collection, please visit https://artistemmaline.wixsite.com/artistemmaline and find her on Facebook and Instagram -@artistemmaline

Special Thanks

Grateful acknowledgment to Mark Mckinney & Co. for the permission to use their band name.

To support Tyler and Victoria's favorite musicians, follow them on Facebook at https://www.facebook.com/MarkMckinneyCo/ to check out their latest music, concert schedule, and gear!

Prologue

Prologue

There are times when I look back on these events and question Victoria's sanity. Was it all a dream? A nightmarish collection of images? Abuelo's records are useless. He was so simplistic in his detail, sterile notes of successful or unsuccessful exorcism attempts. A diary of a scientist, perhaps. She was not as cryptic. I must piece together her story. Sing about it. The story of her, the story of us. Those of us still left to carry on the mission to push against the darkness and hold on to the light.

I document for the children and wayward travelers to come next. Those who may have the gift to exorcize the demons and call the spirits home. There may never be another that is as powerful as Victoria Hartwell. These are the chronicles of a teenage exorcist.

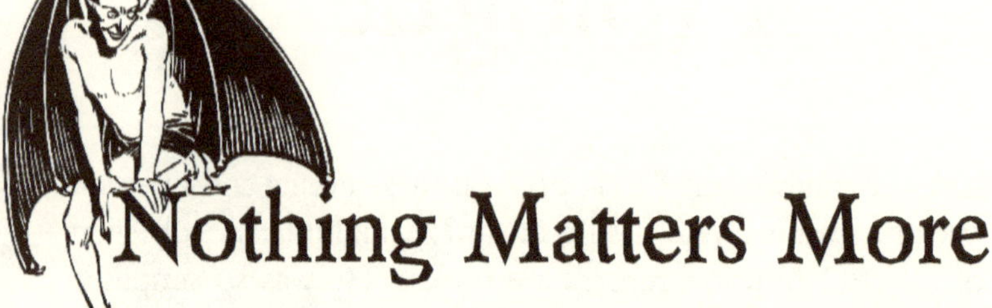

Nothing Matters More

"Let the light enter, the light that conquers the darkness…"
Song Lyric, Portador De La Luz

The house teemed with palpable energy. Victoria knew anger fueled a large part. Any single one of them deserved her lashing out. Instead, she brooded in silence. She crammed her summer wardrobe into her carry bag because not having a timeline for the trip called for a little of everything.

Her bands waved at her from posters on cherry painted walls. Pegs held tickets and itineraries for each stop on the East Coast. Out of loyalty, she switched from random to the summer playlist, and it reminded her what she might have had with Tyler. Abrianna dashed dreams like she did the family portraits along the staircase wall.

Over the mountains, into the woods, to Abuela's house I go…

She tried to sing-song a mood switch, but it only sunk her deeper into her thoughts of how far mountains and woods separated her from Tyler. After knowing him since five, she never thought her friendship with him would turn into something more, yet it was impossible to deny it morphed into a painful, yet beautiful yearning. It wasn't making sense, but she knew tension lived between them now.

But maybe it was only her feeling the intensity of moments. Glancing, she would catch the way their legs fell in step and it somehow brought her comfort in a crowded place. Their arms touched during lunch or how he grabbed her knees and wouldn't let go until she squealed. Maybe "best friend vibes" only, and she didn't want to get it crossed.

What if he met someone new? He was too gorgeous to stay single for long.

Her snap dinged, and the pic made her smile. He sent a side shot of his Cook's shake and guessed it contained his summer grape special. His braided hair peeked around the corner of the cup of goodness.

Since it's easier to blame, she pointed her mind toward Abrianna. Her ridiculous tirade the past six months of self-harm and mutilation caused a fracture in the fault line. Just because her thirteen-year-old sister needed to go to a treatment center up North, canceling her own plans was unnecessary. Victoria posed in front of Mark Mckinney & Co.'s poster and snapped a pout face. They'd miss the first three shows on the tour card.

Tyler got his license that spring, and all they talked of was traveling up and down the East Coast in his VW van like 70s hippies after their favorite bands and even found his grandfather's old atlas and highlighted the roads to take them to the amphitheaters. Tyler purchased the tickets, and his older sister finished a quick summer session from UNC Pembroke and agreed to serve as an official chaperone.

Everything ruined because little sister-girl went wild.

She took a framed picture off her desk. Victoria and Abrianna were two years apart. Both wore crowns of natural, long curly hair, the kind that girls envied but every girl who had it understood how hard it was to tame without a professional hot iron. Their soft brown skin was without blemish, and their eyes were the color of caramel apples, with the granny smith showing through the spaces where the candy didn't melt.

How many times did she hear she shouldn't be singing backup but front and center? Random strangers asked were they models or actresses or told they looked like the younger version of Roselyn Sanchez? Countless. Victoria would redirect any shower of praise to her sister-girl, who seemed to swell at any attention thrown her way.

They had the future planned out. Victoria figured she would never grow to model stature with her five-foot-two frame, but Abrianna had time to stretch into the long-legged beauties of the runway. If she couldn't join them, she would design instead. Victoria made the outfits they were wearing in the picture. Her pale-yellow summer dress, a 50s pattern she loved to copy, complimented the turquoise blouse she single-stitch sewed for her sister. Abrianna loved to pose for her and would twirl and walk the imaginary path of their living room on many nights. She stood stone still for pinning without fear of being stabbed.

Where did those days go? Who beats along the walls next door?

Not her sister. Not anymore. Abri made the house shake.

Her parents' frustrated voices rose above the music.

Adoria Hartwell said, "Did you not call that exterminator back? These spiders are all over the freaking place."

Gideon replied, "I did, hon. Good God, can you just relax. They're just garden spiders. They will be here on Tuesday. We have more important things going on here than your arachnophobia if you haven't noticed."

"We wasted four hundred dollars on that stupid bug contract the first go around. I can't stand this house. Maybe it's the house. It's not her. I feel it's more than her. Can Victoria hurry, so we can leave? I need to get out of here."

"You're taking her. I'm not riding in the car with her for eight hours."

Adoria shrieked. "This has gone too far. She is your Mija, for Christ's sake. She needs you. I'm taking Victoria off to Abuela's house. We have already discussed this."

A trail of Spanish cursing blasted the air, and Victoria turned the volume up even higher. Her parents argued now about every little thing, the television, the spiders that seemed never to leave, the discipline that wasn't working, and the unlucky draw of Abri in a closed space. Her change from innocence to something twisted happened overnight. Who could not fear it?

It wasn't physical because that would've been the easiest to label. Her Mami was the official household website doctor and diagnosed a brain tumor. Abrianna underwent every scan, probe, and prod known to man within the first month.

But the voices called out to Abri, and at the heart of dinner, we would watch her turn her head and answer toward space.

I know. It's coming. I'm ready.

The crawling across the carpet wasn't the least bit humorous in the middle of watching a movie, and family time became nonexistent when Abri decided she would break a cherished object at every mention of a new bonding time activity.

Her antics were on the fringes of bizarre. The cutting sliced deeper, and the scars didn't heal. A rebellious phase born from hormones and cyberbullying she received during her seventh-grade year. So, it turned to a mental and emotional diagnosis when nothing else added up, which led to the all-inclusive stay at Cambion Heights Health and Wellness Center in Massachusetts.

Tyler went live in *Hangouts* for the third time that day, faking bathroom breaks to catch a call with her.

"Chick, listen. We have to figure this whole mess out. Is there room for me in that bag? I can become a contortionist. If I met your Abuela, I'm sure she would love me. She wouldn't mind if I popped up over the weekend, right?"

"No chance. It's a four-hour drive to Asheville anyway."

"Hours mean nothing. I'm the man that is kidnapping you for our tour deluxe, the musical journey that begins in 20,167 minutes, to be exact."

"Tell me you have an app for that."

"Why should I?" Tyler was the genius between them.

Sometimes she hated Hangouts because facial expression control was not her best suit. It was easier to text when emotions boiled.

Her heart hammered in her chest as she flipped over the phone and whispered, "I need you every hour."

"Every hour of every day," his voice softened.

"Promise me this will work out okay." *Promise me you won't find somebody else in my absence,* she wanted to say more than anything.

"With everything I got, I'm putting that down on lock, I promise. No worries, my sexy Puerto Rican princess."

"Oh, stop that! I'm worried you're mad about not going to see the bands. Why did they change their minds and not just let me go with you?"

"Girl, please. I know it's not your fault. You can't control the authorities. Besides, with you not around, I'll just add extra shifts and throw down the patties at the establishment, saving up that minimum wage to buy the gas to bring you home."

"Hey, you need a goal, something to work for." She tried to smile at him but knew tears were about to break free. Better to keep face muscles still as possible. "I have to go." She pointed behind her, "Can you hear them?"

Victoria turned the music off and held the phone towards the door. The ensuing argument partnered with the low growling voice was unsettling her nerves to a breaking point. Anyone would have thought someone penned a pack of Dobermans in the room except the Hartwell's owned none.

"That's insane right there," he answered. "I can't imagine it."

"And this world I live in is going crazier by the minute. Nothing seems to hold me down but you."

Tyler said, "Go write that down. That's a good line for a song."

But it wasn't a line for a new song. It was the truth.

The door swung open with a fierce swoosh, and her Mami said, "Get your things. It's time."

Victoria said goodbye to Tyler, grabbed her two carry bags, and slung her book bag over her shoulder. Passing by Abri's room, she blinked back the tears as she heard moans through the closed door. Regret pinned and needled at her heart for everything she couldn't do. This was more than her. Beyond what she could even understand.

"Is she going to get better?"

Victoria grabbed the doorknob and chills coursed through her body. Her Mami stood by the staircase and refused to move any closer. The shamefaced look spoke a cocktail of fear, confusion, and hopelessness.

Instead of lying, she said, "I don't think that's a good idea. Abrianna isn't in the best of moods today."

Victoria could not ignore the beast sounds. Abri crouched, bruised knees extended outward on the pink-cushioned window seat, hands limp, palms facing up as if asking for candy. Her matted hair clung against her reddened face. The scar might not heal across her brow and be a permanent reminder of the time she tried to gouge her own eye. Her face turned upwards to Victoria, nose raising higher in the air as if to sniff out her identity.

Don't you know me? I'm the one that used to sing you to sleep. I rode you on the handlebars. We fed notes through our closet door so you could learn how to read in Spanish and in English.

Abri squatted, rocked back and forth with her fingers spread wide, and dug at the carpet for balance. The guttural noise was so unnatural with a deep, hissing tone it sounded mixed in a recording studio. Not from Abri.

"Are you ready to burn? You will burn, you know. You and your secret lover. I will see to it, yes, I will. Watch and see you burn, burn, burn. And all the ashes will float up, up, up, and away. Let Tyler enjoy his grape shake while he can. It will be hot where he is going."

Victoria slammed her bags down, fingernails digging in clenched fists. Whatever had leeched itself upon Abri, a disease, a tumor, a manipulative trick, she wanted to beat it out of her.

The panting escalated, and her voice creaked like a hinge of an old door, "Do it. Hit her. Hit her good. Hit her hard. You know you want to. Punch her in her ugly face."

Was this outlandish drama a show for attention? If so, she should have won an Academy finest for the creepiest performance by a young actress.

Victoria broke. "You get better. You stop whatever you're doing. They will figure this out, and then you'll come back, Abri. Do you hear me? Before you tear us apart."

Abri's eyes narrowed into dagger slits. A cracked smile broke across dry lips, and her voice sounded doll-like, "That is the point, the point, the point. That is the point, to tear you apart."

Her Mami pulled her from the threshold and slid the lock in place. A new addition to the house. No other interior door needed one.

Only the one.

Was it for Abri's safety or their own?

"It's time. Now, go hug your father. It might be awhile."

Victoria almost asked how long. She caught her words and reeled them in with Abri's condition now sealed in her mind.

Gideon Hartwell paced the den floor, his hair disheveled, patterned tie out of sorts, behaviors reflective of six months of restless sleep if any at all could be had in a place echoing knocks and scratches in the night. He held the bottle of sleeping pills in his hand. It would be the only way he could get Abri secure in the car without her biting him. She shuddered at the thought of Abri grabbing the wheel during a drive. Her outbursts harmed herself. Anyone. Eight hours did make for a long trip, and she figured he planned to survive it somehow.

He said, "Vic, you take care of yourself. Did you carry your songbook?"

So many thoughts crammed her mind, she couldn't think of what to say that would matter other than, "I love you."

"I love you, too, Doodlebug. I know this has disrupted your life and your summer, but know we had no other choice. Sometimes we have to make sacrifices, and this is one of those times."

She held her breath, and with a heavy exhale asked, "Are you sure this place can help her?"

His eyes switched from her face to the floor.

She continued, "You know I could stay here and take care of everything? Tyler and I already have the tickets and..."

"Don't even think about it, young lady. Those plans have to change, and it's beyond our control. Abuela needs some good ol' Vic time, anyway. It's been years. I bet you'll get some great writing done out there, smack in the middle of nature. They say it's good for the soul."

His "they say" comments again. Who were "they" anyway? They were getting on Victoria's last nerve, too.

Gideon grabbed Adoria's cheeks and kissed her. After all the arguments since New Year's, it seemed like they would file papers, not kissing like she wasn't even in the room.

Victoria heard him whisper, "I'll see you soon enough, my love."

Adoria was not as savage as she tried to portray. Her hands were unsteady on the steering wheel, knuckling it as she hunched over to catch her breath and emotions to regain composure. Her tears mirrored Victoria's, which shimmered with golden flecks of light against her cheeks in the bright light of the sun.

Victoria started kindergarten without her mother, and that was the last time her Mami ran to Abuela's. Memories lingered of hiding under the kidney-shaped table and Tyler putting his arm around her when she missed her smell. Now, she was crying for leaving Tyler, for a summer of stolen music, and most of all, for a sister who might not make it back.

Her eyes lingered over his house. The white picket fence stood out like wholesome goodness on a street where neighbors seldom waved or used porch swings. The red door beckoned anyone inside to a glass of sweet tea and a warm smile. She only needed to slide through the slat in the fence to the tent he set up in the corner yard for when the house got too crazy, and she needed an escape.

They almost kissed there in March. They were sharing a headphone, listening to Mark McKinney & Co., Tyler's favorite band, sing *Nothing Matters More*, while she leaned against his neck. His cologne no longer just a smell of him but it somehow turned to an intoxicating draw.

Victoria turned her face against the window, the air conditioning blowing her hair, sticking strands to her wet face. Dark clouds formed in the distance. A nasty summer storm brewing sent apprehensive shivers through her already overcharged system. Heat thunder crackled. The radio blared louder, and Salsa music tried to erase the trace of sadness trying to form a chrysalis around her heart.

Music chased the demons away. If only life could be that easy, she would have mastered the art. Instead, she let the tears reflect the patterns of rain pelting against the pane. Feeling more lost as the miles clicked on the odometer.

The shak-shak of the new song rattled her senses, "Deja que la luz entre, la luz que conquista la oscuripapi."

She closed her eyes and prayed for the first time in a long while, copying the way Tyler would burst out as if he were talking to her but then his words would direct her to some guy in the sky instead, "Lord, if you're listening, let there be some end to this. Let this be over soon."

Victoria didn't realize she spoke her prayer aloud until her mother said, "Amen."

Those were the last words spoken as they made their way to the Casa de la Abuela. There was nothing left to say.

Shards of Broken Glass

Adelita Hernandez Ortega held an oversized butterfly umbrella in one hand and a lantern in the other as welcome. The glow of the lights streaked across Victoria's vision along with the fireflies that danced near the ditch line. From what she gathered by her parents, Abuela bordered between eccentric, ultra-religious, and was a bit on the flashy side.

"Adori! Mi hija! Necita!"

When her papa passed on a part died with Mami, and so did the family connection they had to the homeplace.

Adoria stood with her while the music blared from the system. Victoria stayed in the car and watched them dance in the rainfall. The tension seemed to erase from her mother's face, a softness returned, and she swore she saw a tiny bluish hue hover for a moment between the two. Maybe a lightning bug or two.

Victoria hoisted her bags on her hip and made her way to the cabin's porch. They soon followed her, locked tight in an embrace, legs close like a three-legged race.

"You shouldn't have kept away this long, Adoria. I have missed the bringing in of the years."

The screen door popped with an eerie screech and knocked Victoria's heel of her Converse. "Hello, Abuela."

"Hello. Hello. Come here, Necita, por favor."

Victoria stood close to her grandmother, and her gentle face calmed her. Abuela put her wrinkled, yet soft hands to cup her cheeks. With butterfly kisses, she danced across the bridge of her nose and swept her hair away.

"Such a beauty, you are, my child, just like your mother but with the fighter spirit, I see."

Abuela whisked her into the kitchen, and she followed the large hips that swished the flowered print dress back and forth with a rhythm of its own. Like flowers on a summer day catching wind.

Abuela mumbled a few words, but Victoria caught her whisper, "The Conqueror. It's time you arrived here."

Victoria glanced at her mother and raised a questioning brow.

Her mother said, "Your name means conqueror, Victoria. Your Abuela named you."

Abuela continued the tour, while Victoria only wanted to find a bed and lie in it.

Her voice lowered. "Do not enter here. This room was your Abuelo's study. Stay clear, or you will be sorry. Dois mio."

She crossed herself and stepped toward the door in front of the study. "This is you."

The bedroom walls were pine knotted wood, and Victoria ran her hands along with the patterns and found a sheep and a broken fence in the grain. Quilts lined the bed with large throw pillows thrown across the center. Cedar from the hope chest and sage wafted through the room. Candles flickered a soft glow on the stained walls to cast distorted dark faces and stretched themselves out in odd shapes.

A small desk nestled in the corner wore a soft lamplight, no television, and no computer. Her songbook would be her lifeline. She could have an uninterrupted, focused time on her music. She could turn this pain into angst lyrics worthy of the playlist for Junior year talent show.

Victoria asked, "Internet?"

"No account. Why bother," Abuela replied. "No one can track my IP address that way."

Her Mami leaned in and whispered, "When I get back home, the first thing I'll do is change the service plan to 4G. Just be patient for one day. You at least deserve an upgrade for what you've been through."

We deserved a rewind to six months ago. A do-over. The lottery. A dream vacation. Hope.

She could hear the faint conversation carry through the cabin. Her Mami tried to switch the subject from Abri to no avail. Taino music charged the atmosphere and allowed her to escape from reality. She realized she had one thing in common with her mother.

She snapped her bear claw quilt tucked on the rocker to Tyler. "How quaint."

He replied with a picture of his scuffed boots. "Need me to come to stomp some mountain critters?"

A framed verse beckoned beside the bed. "… And they brought unto him all sick people that were taken with divers diseases and torments, and those which were possessed with devils, and those which were lunatick, and those that had the palsy; and he healed them. Matthew 4:24."

Victoria snapped. "Nice to see before you close your eyes, huh? Can you say creepy!"

She was sure Tyler knew the very next verse connected to the one in the frame. She turned the frame to face the wall and unpacked the rest of her bags.

Victoria found her way back to the hub of the house by the smell. Delivery boxes were the new normal since they had to devote more time to calm Abri.

She overheard the word months.

"Maybe two to three months, mi amore. She starts back in August, so before the opening day, I'm sure."

"Are you talking about Abri's stay at the mental hospital?"

"It's a wellness center," her mother corrected. "And I was talking about you and your return to Raleigh."

Victoria held her hand out to catch the wall, and the thump of the acceleration of her heart created a drumbeat in her ears. "Mami …"

"I'm sorry, Vic. We have a situation with Abri we have to handle now. Your safety is a high priority, and that means you must stay here for the time being. Trust me."

Abuela stepped in. "Angelita, you will bring light back here in these lonesome woods."

Victoria said, "Light on shards of broken glass." Trembling, her voice seemed far away. "Tyler expects us to go on the tour. Can we still go? He spent hundreds of dollars on the tickets for the three of us."

Victoria tried not to listen to the plans. The tunnel echoed as she ran down to escape the room she stood in. The situation of her life looped her right back to feet planted before them.

Abuela cooed, "Ah, this can be salvaged someway. If it settles down up North, let her get a few concerts in at least."

"And if it doesn't, and she is out there without protection?"

"Mami! Tyler and I are best friends! We want to see the bands. Besides, I've had plenty of opportunities to do that back home! Is that what this is all about? Do you not trust me?"

Abuela rubbed the cross necklace around her neck as she spoke, "That is not the protection she speaks of, Necita. Now, come. Let's eat. The pork will turn cold."

They busied themselves and left her by the dinner table.

The chorus repeated, "Months without him. His love will turn cold."

There was yet another part of her life she could not control, so like a robot, she sat down at the table and let them serve her. Up and down movements of her arm. Swallow. Repeat, as she listened to the drumbeats growing louder.

Months without him
his love will turn cold
Without ever knowing
or without being told
The feelings were growing
but the heart will grow dim
Months without me and him

Lyrics toyed with her emotions and pleaded to grace a page in her songbook. She refused their request and only let them stick to tar coat the sides of the core. Victoria dismissed thoughts of running away because Tyler wouldn't go for it, Mr. Never Break Rules. How much was she going to sacrifice?

The words of her Papi sat beside her at the empty seat. "I know this has disrupted your life and your summer, but know we had no other choice. Sometimes we make sacrifices, and this is one of those times."

Deceit crushed her like falling rocks of an avalanche. Nothing mattered more to her than Tyler and having to tell him the news buried Victoria under boulders she was too weak to lift.

****

The way Abuela asked about Abri's condition was downright like a symptomatic transcriptionist, a nurse taking notes. Victoria understood where the backseat doctor syndrome in the family originated.

Abuela repeated, "Noises? Voices?"

Her mother closed within herself the more the questions fired, and Victoria nodded. "Yes, through the night they get worse."

"What else have you noticed that's strange?"

Victoria's nose crinkled at the thought. "The smell is just putrid. I can't explain it, like rotted animal meat days old on a counter."

She asked, "Do knocks come in threes?"

Victoria shuddered. How did her grandmother know?

Adoria cut in the line of questioning, and it was obvious she had enough. Her voice sounded detached, rehearsed.

"Yes, it's a mental health issue, maybe bordering on an early onset of Schizophrenia. I thought for sure it was a brain tumor. Gideon just thinks it's a phase. The treatment center will run further tests, and who knows what they find. I might never get my baby back, but I believe if hope can be found it's there."

"Don't say such things, Adoria. Christ can heal all things and make them new. We only find hope in Jesus. The place you're sending her to is just a band-aid. You should've sent her here first to let all of us look at her."

Victoria glanced around the room to glimpse "all of us," but only pictures of her grandfather lived on.

Victoria said, "Even though Papi said they say nature is good for the soul, I think breathing forest air isn't going to rectify the soul problem Abri's fighting."

Abuela asked, "Well, what do you think it is?"

Victoria's skin tingled. It was the first time anyone had asked her opinion about the whole ordeal since it began. She was glad for the opportunity to speak her mind.

"She is doing it all for attention. Abri isn't the best at making friends and had some bullying going on last year. She is creating this hysteria, and it started when she found that strange girl online. She met up with that Rachel girl from the private school. It's like the Salem Witch Trials. Call her mom. See if she is doing this foolish mess, too."

Abuela gasped and crossed herself and dug her tiny fingers in her Mami's shoulders. "Adoria, please tell me you did not let Abri befriend someone you don't know? It is a must we keep our circle small. A reason we don't trust outsiders. You know what that could mean."

Adoria rolled her eyes, acting five again. "I can't judge their friends or what they chose to do. The girls are free to be friends with whoever they want. I'm not like you, Abuela."

Abuela leaned over, her fingers massaging her temples. "You should be. The stealer of joy creeps around dark recesses and every corner to attack. And he has struck at the heart of this familia once again. It is time we strike back. Dios mio, ten piepapi de nosotros."

Her mother replied, "No. We do no such thing. You're talking foolishness. Gideon is on his way to the treatment center. She'll get the medical help she needs. This spiritual mumbo-jumbo isn't infiltrating my household. You know I don't believe in that crap, and I'll not have you shoving your religion down my daughter's throat this summer, and she comes home some holy roller. You're not allowed to discuss your past or your faith with my children, or I'll take her home with me now."

Abuela said, "Whether you believe, He believes in you. And so, as the light exists, so does the dark. Evil has taken your child, Adoria. I pray someone removes the scales from your eyes before it's too late to save her soul and everything you hold dear."

Her eyes pierced me as she spoke. I wasn't sure if she was talking about Abrianna or me. The way she wanted to speak more but refrained told me it might have been a warning to the both of us.

Every Hour of Every Day

Gideon pulled up to the gated center. He held the printed materials against the windshield to compare the two and wondered if it was the right place. He had come too far to turn back, so he flashed his paperwork to the guard. Everything was in order. His muscles tightened in his chest to leave her here alone. Whatever happened to Abrianna stole the bit of nerve he had left.

"You have arrived on time. Good. We have prepared for weeks for her coming. Follow me."

The man in the long white coat had a voice so cool, clipped, and directive. Gideon chalked it as the detachment necessary to work with patients like these. Wait, like her.

A burly orderly lifted Abrianna from the backseat like she weighed a penny. She opened her eyes at the stirring, but instead of questioning where he brought her, she smiled a sweet-toothed smile then fell upon his chest back into her dream world.

A nurse with dark eyes cooed lullabies and hush little baby as his mind whirled with the emotions of the past months.

Gideon, unnerved by Abri's reaction, trying to pass it off as disorientation, said to no one in particular, "You might want to hurry it up because of the sleeping pill. It will wear off soon."

"Just what we want to happen," replied the doctor. "No fear. I hear what you're thinking but she won't hurt any of us. She'll be like family soon enough. You will see."

After the intake paperwork, Gideon felt the haze of the place. The dimly lit corridors were too white for his taste.

Everything bleached. The tiles, the walls, the uniforms, the equipment. His daughter was once an artist before she changed. She loved the playfulness of color and the mixture of paints, experimented hours as she dabbled her tiny fingertips in watercolors. He hated the thief who stole color from her. The joy. Life.

A new doctor joined the group who he knew to be Dr. Amon, the director who specialized in cases like Abrianna's, towered over his frame by at least six inches. His eyes fluttered, like shutters with a broken off switch and was more ominous in person than their video conversations. Gideon's pulse quickened, and his hand shook through his hair.

God, should I leave her here? Or do I just need a pot of coffee, a vacation, my wife back...

After a few minutes of paced steps, Dr. Amon's grave voice echoed along the hall. "She is secure."

Something from it hurt Gideon's ears or maybe a headache inched its way into his skull. He had enough to stress about. The months devastated their finances, and he would hate to see the bill when it arrived in the mail.

"When will we find out any news?"

"Time will tell us what we desire to know. We'll bring her to her full potential, that is a guarantee." The doctor's jaw twitched.

A black spider skittled across the floor, catching his attention. It must have been a wayward traveler in the bag, and he went to stomp it with his foot, but the doctor intervened.

"No need for that. They kill the little things that go creep in the night."

Gideon said, "We have tons of those where this little guy came from. By all means, come and collect them, too."

The doctor took his cell out of his pocket. "Spiders, you say?"

"Have another exterminator coming in next week."

"How about toads or any cats? Questioned the doctor.

"No, just spiders. That's enough to make my wife want to move out of the house and burn it to the ground."

He finished his text. Gideon couldn't help but lean over to catch the line. "Check her bag for spiders."

He was sure they would find some.

"As we discussed prior, there will be no contact between family and patient. We have work to carry out, and progress takes privacy. It will be thorough and intensive, but I promise you this, she will become our number one priority. Any day you want an update, contact the lead nurse on her case." He handed Gideon a card.

Gideon just stood in the hallway, waiting for more. For something, but he didn't know what. An unsettling, not-right feeling washed over him, along with a guilt wave to leave his baby girl in the hands of strangers to do God knows what to her. The doctor excused himself with a nod, glancing into a few rooms as he passed, never turning back to him or to bid him goodbye.

He felt foolish, standing there holding the business card in a now empty corridor. He needed Adoria. Gideon never handled a situation with authority.

Should he demand to see Abrianna one more time before he left? Would she recognize him? Would she care? There was no one to ask, and it was best he went. He wasn't planning on spending any more money than he had to, so a hotel was out of the question. He was driving straight back the way he came.

Gideon turned and walked the hall towards the exit. His curiosity caused him to glance in the rooms. All were children. Poor creatures. One with a shaved head. Another with a cut across the cheek, one had scratched the wallpaper off walls, wads of it hanging from bared teeth. He saw an older boy, with empty eyes rocking in the corner of a padded cell. He couldn't look in any more of the doorways, but he would swear on his life as he passed each door, he heard an echo taunting him. A whisper followed his steps as he made it out to the night and fresh air.

"She is here."

****

Adoria backed out of the driveway, her phone rested against her ear. No doubt she'd called Gideon to get the news about the trip North. Her Abuela approached with tiller and hoe.

She wiped the sweat stuck to deep, creviced lines etching river routes on her face, and spoke in a huff, "Which weapon do you prefer?"

"Huh?"

"Honey, I will teach you a way to find yourself in the garden. Now, pick one and let's get this started."

Victoria admitted peace appeared as the day wore on. The rows were void of weeds, and Victoria recognized great care prepared the soil. She found herself fascinated with the dance of the bumblebees along with the squash flowers as they grew bold on vines. Her grandmother didn't talk much, but her breath panted in irregular beats like a child patting a drum.

"It might be time to close this party down," Victoria took the tiller from her hand. "We have another day to make a row."

Her Abuela took waved her straw brimmed hat towards her for the breeze. "True. We have another task ready for some cultivating. I've worn you out, and now we can chat."

If she wanted to talk about Abri, she didn't know if she could handle it. She preferred to write lyrics. Breathe. She had a new mental exercise from her Mami's self-help book. The brick fit to mortar, the foundation laid. Walls could be built if Abuela put her on the defensive.

They settled in with a tall glass of fruit infused water. The air from the vents pushed overtime, and the sound cranked up through the house.

Abuela leaned forward then back, catching her mouth in poses as she considered the entry point.

Victoria asked, "Can we please not do this?"

Abuela shooed her with the hat, swatting her leg. "I'm relaxing, catching my breath, and sipping on my mango water with my Nieta. A grand time, muy contenta."

Victoria eyed her. "You have something to say, don't you? You're trying to figure out if I will go running to Mami if you do. I won't tell anything to her. She has her burdens to bear."

Abuela said, "Well, that means we can speak straight facts. No more playing these games, I need to hear it from you. Do you believe?"

"Believe?"

"In Christ, our Savior. The Lord. The Holy Spirit. The Trinity. Do I need to go on?"

"I don't talk about religion or politics. It's better to keep my own thoughts to myself. That's how we do things in the Hartwell family."

Abuela snorted. "Ridiculous. Talk all you want. God gave you a voice, and it's time you use it for those who can't speak for themselves. Child, I'm serious. Do you believe in a higher power?"

Victoria had thought little about it. She went through motions without the thoughts of religion or God or that holy roller stuff, as her mother called it. Tyler was a Christian. His family didn't miss church, Sunday or Wednesday nights, and she'd only gone a few times for special events.

"I don't know."

Abuela surprised her with a smile. "That's a start. At least you didn't turn up your nose and curse me out, calling me a crazy, old bat."

Victoria answered, "I'd do no such thing. Just because I don't understand it all, doesn't mean I have never had questions or doubts. I mean, my friend, Tyler, he believes it. If he does, it makes me wonder if it could be true. I trust his judgment, just never experienced it."

"That's fair enough." Abuela asked, "So, this Tyler, he sounds like someone I'd like to meet. You love him, right?"

"Abuela! He's my best friend. He lives next door and…"

She smacked her lips and puckered up. "And you love him. Heed my warning. Just be careful. You need all your senses in the months to come. Getting caught up with some boy might need to be placed on the back burner. We have more work to do with you, yet."

"He isn't on any burner, nowhere near the kitchen, even."

The conversation didn't once turn to Abri, instead, she sprawled out on thick carpets surrounded by an album collection to die for.

When Tyler had the chance to call, she had the sudden urge to cry but willed herself to hold it in, and she allowed his animated voice full of stories of the day distract her long enough to redirect. She lay in bed and listened to the comforting sound of his voice, the actual chirping of crickets by her window, and the last six months toppled on her all at once.

The night would be void of violent screams, no head bangs against her wall. No closet door to creak open when she knew full well it was her sister playing tricks on her to scare her through the connecting passageway between their rooms. She would be in a cabin bedroom, four hours away from home, with an eccentric old Christian woman who poured out anointing oil she had in her hands to bless her after she wished her a good night. Tears of release hit her pillow. She needed this more than she thought.

She prayed as Tyler's voice droned on, *if there is a God, thank you for my Abuela, and for bringing me here.*

As always, they ended their call with the words they spoke to each other last Christmas. "I need you."

His tone lowered, "Every hour of every day."

She loved him, with everything, heart, and soul. She knew she couldn't do this summer void of Tyler's presence and would have to get back home to him. Lyrics played tug of war with her eyelids, and sleep might not win.

Let it be me
Every hour of every day
Let your every night be filled with me in it
Every day makes sense as long as you're in it
And you'll have no peace and quiet
Your heart will start a riot
 and you'll have to
come to me
And I'll show you
what real means
I am ready. I am here.

And I am waiting.
I am worn. I am broken.
Anticipating.
For the day I get to see you again.
I am here.
I need you every hour of every day.

It Began with Us

The preparation brought such a busy time and tremendous satisfaction. When her arrival date drew near, the doctors and nurses on staff for many years, those who came respected in Demonology, now shriveled in fear, balled themselves up like infants in the darkness that settled over the conference space like a vaporous gas. They heated conversations and fiery debates hit earthquake proportions. Was it the appointed time? Those that asked withered in the room's corner.

"Silence," Dr. Silas Amon barked, his teeth bared like a dog on the attack. "You will not question my authority on this matter. It will be time soon enough. The signs are there."

He flipped the slides and projected her case notes along the white wall.

Patient Case File: 666

Name: Abrianna Manuela Hartwell (Image 1: Recorded before Infestation Period Christmas 2017)

Age: 13 (DOB: January 1, 2006)

Admission Date: June 8, 2018

Family History: Adoria & Gideon Hartwell, parents; One sibling: Victoria Elizabeth

Religious affiliation: None

Medical History: Appendix removed, age 7, tonsils age 11; high blood pressure and stroke of grandfather; mother suffers from clinical depression; no other psychological illnesses reported; missing records

Allergies: Shellfish; bee stings (EpiPen protocol for anaphylactic episodes)

Infestation: Approximately 3 months

Recording of Infestation Account (Group Therapy Session #3)

Oppression: Ongoing

*Images 2-8:** Intake pictures of body markings, gouged eye evidence; eye dilation minimal (June 8)

*Image 9:** Urine in puddles in Room 7 (June 9)

*Image 10:** Spider crawling out of the ear (Group Therapy Session #5, June 10)

*Image 11:** "Join" carved between shoulder blades (June 11, 3:33 a.m.)

Recordings of Oppression (ongoing)

No one dared to speak as the images flashed. Unfathomable to believe after all the research conducted of child cases they had mistreated, the one arrived. The time had come. Each new image caressed their senses, and they moaned in ecstasy with a rush of the thrill of that knowledge.

Silas Amon was the most pleased among them and received the greatest reward for his incredible work ethic and dedication to this task. It had been his life's purpose for mere existence to serve the Master and find the one vessel that could host the source of the legions of devils who waited to bring about the turn. Those who did not fit the profile in every cell along the thirty-three-bed facilities at Cambion succumbed to be the receiver to a lesser demon who would soon become a servant when the possession occurred.

He relished the thought of how impressed the families of those he soul captured commended them on the one-to-one staff, patient ratio, and brought in the highest rates for service three years running. Five-star internet reviews, not to mention the awards and payments made over the years for quality care. Little did those ignorant humans know those cured were out and incognito for the time for the reckoning. They lived among the sinners and liars, blended in with societal ills brought on by deceit and destruction. Despair heavy at work and devils masked well in times like these.

Silas Amon surveyed the room as he licked his lips. His fire radiated through the gray, tailored suit. Easy for manipulation, these sadistic fools with a thirst for power. If only they understood what was to come.

He drew his thoughts away from the future and pulled up the recorded girl's confession. The earliest medicine regiment provided to the patients comprised sodium thiopental, no need to waste precious time in the so-called Group Therapy sessions with those little brats who tried to play tough. Relationship icebreakers were not ridiculous precepts of Cambion, tapped out abilities of hosts and the condition of the bodies for the attachment became the top priority upon admission. Understanding their transition from infestation to oppression was essential for identification and documentation purposes.

It helped .to speed things along, once they pinpointed the weaknesses of those pitiful boned children that could crack at the slightest mention of how their families would be next. That did it.

Family. The institution was overrated. At least he could stamp out some of them from bonding again. Fixed souls reunited under the guise as the devils lived within as manipulated pets.

Dr. Amon pronounced, "One day the world will know how it all began. That it began here. With us."

The video played. He watched it countless times, for hours on end just to hear it retold, burned it into his memory and could feel the words as they scurried through veins. He didn't mind it one more time. He would have to put up with the moans of the others in the room. It added an element that should have grated against Amon's last thread of nerve but brought him great pleasure. *They recognize it is because of my doing; they are worshipping me for this.* He reveled in that, for the time being at least. Soon, it would all be her.

He focused his attention back to the video projection and increased the volume. "Tell us," chanted the five children in the surrounding circle, "Tell us when he called to you. Where did it happen?"

Abrianna's weariness framed her delicate features. She had been through so many torturous experiences, so much more than the others to come ever would. The exercises and group sessions broke what last of her will she held.

Silas clasped his hands together, enthralled with her union of the One. He didn't know it would be so easy for her to tell about the middle of the night, on New Year's, how she and Rachel made their way to the abandoned tobacco barn on the line between Rachel's farm property. Her guardians from the foster care system were drunk from a party. Rachel took the candles from the mantlepiece, ordered her to take the book, and they made their way without anyone to stop them or care. Such a little pet, Rachel. Follows directions well, she does.

The decrepit barn where the lullaby wooed her soul would be a gathering of the reapers. Soon. He let her tell the story and rubbed his chest with deep satisfaction.

Her voice doll-like, twisted with the demonic. "Oh, how I loved the way the clay felt under me as I sat in the circle Rachel drew. I felt wanted. The dirt had a scratchy throat and called me deep into it. My hands rubbed the pebbles mixed with old shards of glass, some rough, some smooth, some cut."

As she spoke, the rapt audience bit their fingers and gnawed at their wrists. The atmosphere charged with intense promise. When the video surveillance caught the spider that crawled from her ear, down the line of her jugular vein, which way to go, front or back, then disappeared down the collar of her shirt, that did the room in. The girl did not flinch or try to push the spider away. She did not shake in fear. So close to being one with him who came to catch fire to the world. So close.

He stopped the video. The initial union of the One and Abrianna would be for him only. They would bear witness to one of the most substantial pieces of evidence Silas Amon would share. His lead nurse forwarded the video feed to 3:36 a.m.

The voice of the demon broke through the predictable moans of the host. Its deep guttural retreat from her evil soul. He spoke prophecy, revenge, an entangled power by the growls of legions escaped from the pits of hell.

"I will set fire to the wood. I will set fire to the wood. It will all go down in flames. No prophet, no Christ, no priest will stop me. I will set fire to the wood."

****

Victoria was alone. Abuela drove down the mountain for supplies, to meet her friends for coffee, and stop by the library for another bag of books. She promised to tidy up the house, but the way Abuela kept it, there was no need.

The peacefulness of the place did wonders for her creativity. Victoria penned three new songs over the week. She knew she wouldn't have the nerve to share them with Tyler because they weren't their typical progressive rock style, these were about love in the sappiest ways. Victoria blamed it on him.

She stopped dead in her tracks. Scratches caught her attention behind the closed door of her Abuelo's study. The off-limits room. Sounds grew louder, this time partnered with a squeak. She volunteered to house clean, and his forbidden study shouldn't have been an exception to the rule. Every spot needed a good dusting off. She checked her watch. Abuela said she would be home around one, and gave her the morning of freedom and exploration. Her curiosity spilled over with the noise that wafted through the pine slots of the door and beckoned her to just remove whatever trapped critter was on the other side.

As soon as she released the old latch and swung the door wide, a flying squirrel came near her face, then landed on the picture frame along the wall. Victoria ran for the broom, opened the hall window, and readied her position to coax the adorable, tiny beast to liberty. In all the excitement she still snapped the story out to Tyler, who would never believe she dared to face the creature without even a single scream or peep.

She lowered the window frame and walked along the narrow hallway and stopped to stare at each picture of her grandparents. They held hands, a youthful spirit about them resonated even though the black and white portraits. He had on a plaid newsboy cap and was the dashing kind of handsome. The suit had to be white, cream, or tan.

Abuela was the epitome of a Spanish princess. Her long hair flowed gracefully, wisps caught on camera as if a modeling fan blew in front of her, with a flared skirt in full swing. They had an indescribable glow around them, which could have been filters and flash. Could natural love radiate like that? They loved each other with a deep passion. She wanted this as the cover of her debut album, for sure.

Victoria didn't want to speak or hug Tyler right away. She didn't want a word between them before she caught a selfie, just to see the way they looked together when they saw each other again. Her love for him would continue to be the gravitational force that revolved her world, and she wondered if she and Tyler would have that glow like her grandparents when she captured them in a frame.

Victoria stepped inside the study, clicked on the desk lamp and pulled the drapes to let the natural light in. One window propped open, just high enough to allow the critter in. Mystery solved. The pine branches danced around the window and popped the glass like a mosh pit.

How high was this room? The deceptive one-story cabin from the front of the house hid a second level. There must've been a cutaway in the mountain.

Victoria sat down at her Abuelo's antique roll-top desk. She touched the trinkets and held each one up for inspection. A ceramic angel warrior clasped a sword, heavier than she first thought. Framed verses, an old stitched bookmark in need of a new book to command and a line of fountain pens laid out in a row. There was no dust. It was pristine.

Her Abuela must have kept this room as spotless as the rest to preserve his place. She didn't feel like a trespasser here, almost as if she belonged among the stacks of old newspaper, stamp collection, and his framed fishing lures. Her eyes took in every inch of the room and tried to recreate a man she didn't remember. Her feet tripped over an upturned corner of the red oriental rug. When she went to adjust it, the slats did not match the rest of the floorboards.

Victoria pulled back the faded oriental rug and gasped when she found a door. She lifted it with little struggle, the sound of the old creak let her know it had never been oiled. She drew out her cellphone and flipped on the flashlight. A thin, planked spiral ladder styled staircase led to the mysterious room. She had to. No other option existed.

Victoria lowered herself, one foot at a time, down the unstable ladder steps. If a flying squirrel found her on the top floor, she shuddered at the thought of what could live down in the dark. She pushed that out of her mind. The expectation of greater finds than critters allowed her courage to swell. Tyler would have called her inquisitive since he liked to use fancy vocabulary words to one-up her. She would have just called herself nosy and went about her way.

Victoria flashed her phone to orient herself to her surroundings and looked for light. She caught sight of a metal ball pull string. A soft flickered glow released from an antique lantern fixture. Was this some shrine? Was this to honor her grandfather's memory?

Crosses lined the walls, figures of angels, stone, and wood stood guard in the corners. On a side table, she found a large, black medicine bag filled with glass soda bottles labeled, *Holy Water* with a marker. Anointing oil belts and sage ropes hung from pegs along the foundation boards. A dark cloak suspended from the ceiling on a wire hanger tied to a string.

One wall was cased with books that appeared old as time. A collection worthy of a museum, not a dusty basement, but many with torn covers or sections ripped. *Demon History: Names, Origins, Powers and How to Overcome Each* caught her attention. Books on the battling of good vs. evil were the most prevalent, with more Bibles than Victoria had ever seen housed in one place.

Her grandparent's photographs were in every nook and cranny, and strangers stood beside them, shoulders proud. They held small children that reached out to her grandfather with prayerful type gratitude. Coins and stamps from other countries framed beside photographs of cultures unlabeled, but clearly marked foreign travel.

Were they famous? Did they help these people?

The room was difficult to maneuver through because of the countless statues, cabinets, and Halloween decorations that looked as if they were collected for years on end. They must love that holiday around the Ortega household by the looks of the gargoyles, tombstones, and statues that occupied the room.

Victoria's hairs stood on end to be among the more twisted ones that looked handmade, strewn together with straw and mud, wood, and carved masks with black paint. An angel stood guard without a head, replaced with the skull of a goal. Porcelain dolls lined a shelf along a side of the basement that held yellow cop tape, *Do Not Cross.* One doll with a rose printed dress had a broken arm in a tiny handkerchief sling and a gash across her nose. Victoria could swear it stared at her. If she could gather the courage about her to ask Abuela's permission, she'd get Tyler with that one.

Then, her eyes fell on the front page spread newspaper clipping framed to the paneled wall, **"Dr. Manuel Ortega, Renowned Forensic Psychologist – Modern Day Exorcist, Recounts How God is with Us, Even When Faced with the Evil Within."**

She leaned into the ladder, and she sat down on a plank. *Oh, my God. Abuelo, an exorcist?*

The dots connected in her brain, and for the first time, it fell into perfect place, flashbacks of the previous six months snapped in front of her like she was at the Charlotte Motor Speedway holding her breath for the last turn.

But when she caught sight of her grandfather's journal entitled, *Symptomatic Episodes of the Demon-Possessed,* she knew he would confirm her worst nightmare. She checked off with firm confirmation inside her soul and counted as she read aloud his list:

1.Knockings in three, mocks the Trinity
2.Aversion of sacred objects or acts of communion, prayer, or holy water
3.Unexplained marks
4.Putrid smells
5.Voices (Animal, Foreign, Guttural)
6.Abnormal twisted weak bodies
7. Unnatural strength or abilities
8. Devilish behavior uncharacteristic of personality

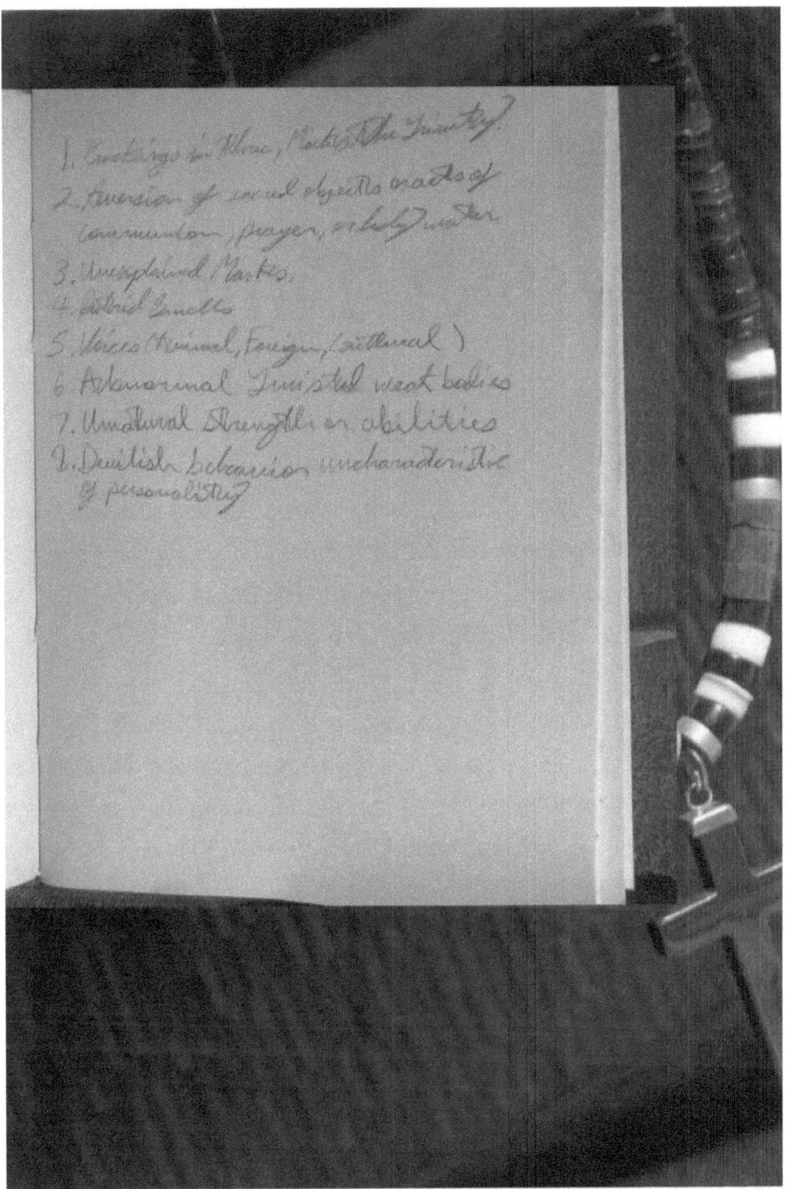

Something possessed Abrianna. Her sister fought against a demon.

Everyone else would think she'd lost her mind. Her parents would send her to that treatment facility along with Abri. Tyler would tell his family, and they would never let them hang out together again. She looked around at his secret room, his exorcist study, and she knew Abuelo would believe her if she told him the signs. If only her Abuelo were still alive.

Who could save her sister now, with a demon welled up inside?

Perfect Timing

*F*ebruary 27, 1976 – The exorcism of the woman was successful. Age, 42, a poltergeist in residence, Instructions to single mother - monthly salt barriers, sage, prayer readings, baptize all members of the household. Sixteen days, duration. The name was Sulak.

March 8, 1982 – The exorcism of the elder was successful. Age 82, ended in the death of the body but life eternal with Christ. Soul was won, but the body was weak. Instructions to children – cleanse the home, baptize any left members and bring to faith, sell, honor the memory of all the days before the possession, and how she fought to be free of the bonds of evil. Two days, duration. The name was Abaddon.

May 5, 1994 – The exorcism of the man was not successful. Age 23, called in Jacoby for assistance. As of date, still possessed. Turned over to a psychiatric facility in Maine. The name is unknown. No further records.

October 31, 1998 – The exorcism of the youth was successful. Age 13, the day of Bar mitzvah (note importance) – simultaneous possession, twins. No recollection of paranormal experiences. Instructions to parents – examine consistent prayer life, baptism by faith. 13 days duration. The names were Badgala and Lillith.

August 22, 2000 – The exorcism of the child was successful. Age 7, in God's perfect timing He made her whole again, with no recollection of the attacks. Instructions to parents to continue spousal counseling for healing, *the child will be exceptional mentally with no record of wrongdoings. Spiritual covering to baptize those of the entire household in the faith, recommended at first opportunity. Four weeks, duration. The name was Jezebel.*

Hours passed since Victoria first discovered the basement office. The journal books pulled from the shelf held taped notes, newspaper articles, appearances at universities, photographs paper-clipped, and demon possession case notes that spanned throughout her Abuelo's lifetime.

She counted four decades of his life's work. Same story, different target. Demons had no respect for a person. Devils had no prejudices, just soul hungry for the weak. Some accounts were elders, middle-aged, the twenties, teens, and the seven-year-old was the youngest she found so far. It was male and female. Black and white. It was the believer and the non-believer alike.

Those that were once like her.

Victoria pulled out a small, leather-bound Bible from the shelf. It felt warm and fit in her palm. It was a worn copy, marked with lines, highlighted, and cared for with loving reverence.

God, are you real? You must be real to fight this evil because it would overtake us all if you weren't in charge.

She needed Tyler without telling him what she had learned of her family history.

She started off the thread of messages. "Don't laugh, okay. It's a legitimate question I'm about to ask?"

"Don't ask me the color of my boxers. We don't speak of those things."

"Hush. Do you truly believe in God?

"Jesus is the way, the truth, and the life. You know how much I love Jesus, Vic."

"I know. But do you believe?"

"Uh, yeah. How can I love what I do not know to be true? My love is on rock, not sand. I believe it all, down to the last drop."

"Everything about it? The whole Bible?"

Victoria flipped through as they talked. She took after her Abuela and reading but ebooked everything she could now, and was on hold for an enormous list of the most popular summer titles. Tyler read nothing other than the Bible that she knew of, anyway.

The phone rang. "The Bible is the best, Vic. Your grandmother working on you, huh?

"I guess."

"I love grannies."

Victoria laughed. "Me, too."

She smiled at the thought of the ritual her grandmother held without fail. Her resting in the recliner, three blankets wrapped around her legs, and her Bible in her lap. The reading glasses would move on and off, the chain rattling as it hit her necklaces when she would nod at something she liked.

"You weren't raised in the church like me, so I know it can be a little overwhelming. For me, it's a part of who I am. Like a part of my name. Tyler Bible-Believing-God-fearing-Jesus-Saves Locklear.

Victoria laughed. "Is that your Native American name? That's catchy."

"Yeah, maybe so."

"I don't know how to talk about these things."

"Ask me anything. If I don't know, I can find it out. I'm from the place where you're asked two things by a stranger, who's your people and where do you church at. Hold on, let me get my Bible. Do you have one? If not, pull up the app."

"I have one now," she answered.

"So, fire away. This is the best Jeopardy round ever."

This isn't a game. My sister's life depends on it.

"What does it mean to mock the Trinity."

"Wow, girl. You start off with the big stuff, with some hypocrisy, don't ya. The Trinity is the belief that God, the Son of God, Jesus, and the Holy Spirit, who Jesus sent as our comforter and guide, as being One and the same. You don't speak against that. It's blasphemy."

"Do you believe God created the world, Tyler?"

"And then there was light. Genesis tells me so."

"So, it's the Bible tells me so defense. But how do you know that you know?"

He sighed. "I just do. It's a feeling. It's there with me like a heartbeat. As real when I touch you. It's the faith in the unseen. Jesus changed my life."

"Have you been baptized? Why get baptized in the first place?"

"Yes, when I was ten. I was younger when I asked Jesus to be Lord of my life. As soon as I was able to read the New Testament on my own, I knew that my next steps had to be the outward showing of faith. My Uncle Bobby actually baptized me in the Lumber River. It's what we did back home. If they helped lead us, they could help clean us."

Tyler's family was originally from Robeson County, but they visited a lot to see his relatives. They were a tight-knit sort, holding on to their cultural traditions and their faith. They also welcomed her as if she were Tyler's sister, a piece of her felt home smack in the middle of their crew.

Her voice trembled, "Do you think you might baptize me one day. I want it to be you."

Tyler answered, his voice thick with emotion, "Any day of the week. Sweet thing, do you believe in Jesus now?"

She knew something changed since she arrived on Abuela's mountain. Hearing her read the beatitudes her first night before bed put her at peace like nothing could, "*Blessed are they which do hunger and thirst after righteousness: for they shall be filled. Blessed are the merciful: for they shall obtain mercy. Blessed are the pure in heart: for they shall see God.*"

Victoria said, "I might be getting there. When Abuela is reading at night, it's not that my ears are listening. It's like my soul is waking up for the first time and paying attention."

"Then it was worth it, then."

"What?"

"You leaving me for the summer. Canceling the concert tour. All of that matters to nothing, compared to your salvation and your eternity. I'll be praying for you. I'm here if you need to talk about it. Anything."

"I know." And she did. There was no doubt.

He said, "I need you every hour."

Victoria brushed the tears that fell without permission. "Every hour of every day."

****

This demon is stronger than any I have encountered. It can receive the crucifix and not mark. Hurry. Bring the arsenal. Soon, Jacoby Wethington

No date was on the note. Just a warning scribbled on yellowed paper, one of many folded in the Bible Victoria still held in her hands since her call with Tyler.

She landed on a verse and read, "Do not let your hearts be troubled. You believe in God; believe also in me."

God, help my disbelief.

She picked up the cross closest to her. It was of a tarnished metal, copper and silver. Victoria turned it over in her hands. Could this crucifix drive out a demon? Did it have some mystical powers since it once belonged to her grandfather?

September 15, 2007.

She wondered what the significance of that date etched into the crucifix. There were no case files that reached that far.

Victoria had closed up the last journal on an April 2007 snapshot of the family. Her father was not in the picture, maybe he was taking it. Her mother was there, and so was her and Abri as a baby. She had no recollection of the day. It was at a dip in the mountain parkway road that allowed for picture taking, so the stretch of the Appalachian Mountains spread out in all their glory behind them.

Was this their last picture together? Her mother would want this. Victoria took a scan with her app and transferred it over to her photos. If she wasn't so caught up in the fascination of her Abuelo's journals, she could have recorded them all to digitize them to show Tyler later. Victoria needed more time to study these. If she took the Bible or the journals with her up the stairs, she would have to risk getting caught, of explaining why she felt compelled to disobey her one wish to stay out of her Abuelo's office.

Guilt washed over her as she flipped through the notes and snapped his diary, Abuelo's personal accounts and she was snapping like some ridiculous paparazzi.

A shuffle of feet and creaking floorboards interrupted her plans.

Abuela's head peeked over the opening in the floor. She crinkled her nose as dust hit her, scanning the room until she caught sight of Victoria.

She smiled, a warmth spreading across her face as if I had won a race, a marathon, or a full scholarship to Duke. No condemnation or disappointment.

Abuela said with great satisfaction, "So you found it. It's about time."

Fear Not

Dr. Silas Amon stared into his eyes with the penlight and banged his head against the plastered wall. *His pupils should have blackened by now.* He no longer allowed them to refer to the patient as Abrianna Hartwell or use her pronouns. In his estimation, any day they would welcome the final transition. Agitation increased, and he accounted that as the tearing away from the soul as if the child thought they could fight their way back. Ignorant humans underestimating the power of the dark side yet again.

Since *he* no longer had an appetite for food, they couldn't risk starvation or dehydration, so IV bags were sustenance enough. Dr. Amon wouldn't allow the body weakened to the point of heart failure nor allow another pound lost, a single muscle to atrophy. He ordered the physical therapist to come and complete the exercises three times a day.

"They've called again," the nurse reported. He didn't refer to them as names either. No, Dr. Dan or Nurse Nancy. They were all lower demons, not worthy of his recall.

Dr. Amon said, "And."

The nurse bit her lip, her voice quivering. "If we do not appease them, they will become suspicious."

"Let them all just die," he answered. Silas Amon lacked the graces of communication or civility.

"I told our strict policy of no parental contact. They signed agreements with the intake packet."

"That should be enough."

"It wasn't. The mother is demanding a diagnosis."

He answered, "Of course she is. Aren't they all? Bipolar disorder, schizophrenia, social anxiety disorder, epilepsy. Choose one."

The nurse grinned. "Oh, it's my turn to play God."

Dr. Amon spat on the floor. Burn marks formed in the saliva. "Don't speak that name in my presence, you imbecile. In front of *him*, no less. You sicken me. You all disgust me with your ignorance and incompetence. You held on to your human too long and are weak because of it. An embarrassment."

She scurried away, head bowed, hands raised because of what would follow. He struck her with the bedside table, pushing her through the corridor.

The verbal attack did not end. "A dishonor to our kind. Useless. Pathetic."

The others came to witness. Something about hatred brought them out as if they were merely taking a stroll at the fair, and since pleasure-seeking entertainment was rare, they piled around in droves.

His right hand, Bathin, stepped in between the strikes. "The sixty-sixth. Need I remind you we do not have the time to recruit and harvest another to replace this reprobate. Let her go. You've humiliated her enough."

Even though the others were rocking with anticipation for the kill, the patients ramming into their doors to break free for a witness – Bathin was right. As fast as his rage began, Silas pulled it back in like an eloquent rehearsal. He pulled on the trim of his suit, adjusting his tie.

"Thank you, my friend. Sometimes their ignorance makes me lose my mind."

Bathin grinned. "Up in here, up in here."

Silas glared at him. "You are not funny. Do you know this?"

"As you tell me, at least once a day."

"I will remind you of this for eternity it seems. Follow me."

"You worried?"

"No, I'm growing impatient. A trip to hell might do me some good."

As they approached his office, he noticed his lead nurse stood by his door.

He couldn't help but growl a low rumbling he passed off as clearing of his throat when in public or around Earthly company. Hundreds of demons fighting within him sounded off as his outrage built again.

"What now?"

"They've called again, sir. They want to know if you have concluded your tests and come to any diagnosis. It's the mother. She is relentless."

He motioned for Bathin to leave him. "Give me the phone. Let me deal with this so it will buy us more time in peace to focus on the transforming hours instead of the threat of parental control or an untimely visit."

He leaned back in his chair, kicking his legs up on the oversized, mahogany desk to settle himself into what he recognized could be one of the long and grueling conversations when a parent first learns of their child's clinical diagnosis.

"Good evening, Mrs. Hartwell. It is nice to accept your call."

****

"Well, hello there, Abuela. I guess you caught me red-handed."

Abuela climbed down with more assurance than Victoria had and stood with her arms crossed over her. "It's been years since I've been down here. I have to hold my chest in."

"Are you okay? Is it the dust? The allergies?"

"No, my nerves dear. You just don't realize the toll this life brought to both of us. I'm holding my heart inside so it doesn't escape from my chest."

Victoria moved the journals back to their place on the shelf. "Let's go on up then. I'm done here."

She raised an eyebrow. "Are you now? Are you sure?"

Victoria nodded. "Not sure about anything. Is all this true, about Abuelo?"

She replied, "It is time we spoke truths in this family. Every truth that sets you free, at least. Every single account, picture, and recording is true."

"Mami never told me about any of this. She claimed he worked as a criminal psychologist in legal trials for serial killers and such."

Victoria also remembered how her mother stated his cases were too grotesque to talk about, and she would change the subject.

"Oh sure, she didn't lead you on. Manuel did that in the beginning of his career and was successful, one of the best in the field. They called him all over the country to crack the toughest ones to solve. But then, that all changed with one case that set your Abuelo apart. His purpose in life, his exorcist role came down to this."

She picked up a small wooden lion. It seemed like a child had carved it with a crude knife. Victoria reached out her hand, ready to take it, but Abuela slapped her hand away.

"Best not to touch the objects in the room, dear. Your faith may not be up to the challenge."

The conversation she just had with Tyler lingered between them. Were these trinkets and statues somehow alive, listening in on her weaknesses and doubts?

"The mother who practiced in the dark arts bought the lion as a gift and passed to her teen. No one knows what spell she put on the carving, maybe she was trying to complete a protection spell. Those who don't know the dangers often fall within the grasp of evil before they can say, "Boo!" and it grabs them ahold."

Victoria held her own heart. The voice inflection did not calm her nerves.

Her Abuela continued. "A demon took over her son. The doctors thought it was epilepsy at first. The symptoms were similar. Then, he told of events in the lives of those he had never met and details too specific to be a coincidence. His mother should have considered it to be a mark of satanic forces at play, but she paraded his newfound gifts and introduced him to Santeria."

"Santeria?"

"It's a form of spirit worship, ritualistic. They didn't heed the warnings of the dark. He killed his first victim as a sacrifice. The second and then the third, he said, because the voices in his head commanded him to do so. He slashed their throats, left them to bleed out on his kitchen floor, then gutted them, eating each of their intestines as soup. What he called a delicacy."

Victoria covered her mouth. "Enough, please Abuela. Spare me the details."

Abuela set down the lion, crossed herself, picked up one of the Holy Water bottles and splashed it against the lion, marked her forehead and made the symbol of the cross on Victoria. "Bendícenos, Dios. Okay, sorry about that. Skip to where your Abuelo comes into the picture. So, they fly him to the Nevada desert. He learned of an old Navajo curse and understood the cultural beliefs where they swore this skin-walker had somehow possessed the son. The mother was now in great pain, for in her mind, and those within her tribe, she had opened up the darkness and allowed it to take her son's soul."

Victoria stared at the lion. She could have sworn that his eyes danced in the dim light. Maybe she and Abuela needed to remove themselves, stop this talk now before she could never sleep again. The nightmare may come to her while she was awake. Like now.

"Can you skip to Abuelo?"

"Patience, dear. So, he tests the boy. He is about your age, with multiple murders behind him. Pure evil. It was not a psychosis, paranoia, or cultural phenomenon. The skin-walker was very difficult to release from the boy. The local shaman was unsuccessful, the homicide department turned to Manuel for answers but refused to release the report, even though they were witness to the transformation. Manuel tricked the animal spirit into showing itself and speaking its name. The rest is history. That case never made it to the light of day. You can't find any of that in the police report, case closed and filed away. No one knows that story, not even your mother."

"Why are you telling me, then?"

"Because you need to believe, Victoria." Abuela sighed and patted Victoria on the shoulder. "I guess it's time to contact some old ghosts."

Her eyes widened, and she gasped. "A seance? I've seen too many of those movies gone wrong. I say let's not. I'll have no part in that!"

Abuela lifted a picture off the wall shelf and handed it over to Victoria. "This is Jacoby, our closest friend. It's time to bring him back from the dead."

Victoria felt for her phone snuggled safely in her pocket. If she called 911, how long would the cops take to get there up to the mountain road? Maybe that was the point of the home in the forest, no one to trace them back here, and they could continue to live out their lives with some normalcy, before the next case.

Her hands itched to take the Bible as Abuela turned to go back up the stairs. Maybe she needed the crucifix, too.

Abuela sensed her hesitation to leave. "Take up what you need, dear. These steps are old, wouldn't want you coming up and down more than needs to be done."

Victoria slid the Bible in her back pocket, grabbed the crucifix and the journals. Abuela dialed the old rotary phone still in use on the wall by the fridge.

Victoria heard a gruff, old voice over the line bark, "Yeah, who is this?"

"Well, you old fart. Wake up. It's well after two."

The startled yell spoke volumes, "Is that you, my Lita, my love?"

"We have a certain situation that needs addressing." Abuela glanced her way.

The man said, "On my way."

"About time you came for a visit, anyway. It's been going on for ten years. You watch too many movies. Faking identities and the sort. And for what, you can't hide from the Lord."

"I know. Shame on me. Don't get started on the guilt trip before my actual trip. It will ruin the reunion."

Abuela whispered, "Bring the arsenal."

Victoria was hypersensitive to everything and caught every word. What had the note in the Bible read? Those same words, but on that torn piece of paper, Jacoby Wethington had asked Abuelo to bring his arsenal.

Victoria watched her pull out the large caldero from the bottom cabinet, and busied herself with cooking as if the conversation that just occurred never happened. It seemed not to phase her one bit, but as she glanced at the floor all she could imagine was the skin-walker lying there with their intestines pulled like a sausage on a string for the cannibalistic ritual. She shook her head as if to force the images to clear.

"My spaghetti was always Jacoby's favorite. He didn't know I snuck a little sofrito in it."

Victoria tried to steady her voice, "Abuela, you put sofrito in everything."

"You notice everything, don't you dear? Have no fears about Jacoby, he comes across as a Copperhead, but he is more of a Rat Snake if you ask me."

Victoria said, "Does he shapeshift into an animal?"

Abuela smirked. "Oh, he would wish it so. Use to always say he wanted to be a werewolf, crazy old man. No, Neita. He is of the faith. He is one of us."

Victoria sat at the kitchen table and pulled the Bible from her pocket.

"Turn to Isaiah 41:10. Let that one sit with you while I mix up the sauce."

Victoria turned to the table of contents. Old Testament, check. She read aloud, "Fear not, for I am with you; be not dismayed, for I am your God; I will strengthen you, I will help you, I will hold you up with my victorious right hand."

"Victorious. That's your birth verse. I didn't name you Victoria for nothing. You might want to start memorizing some power verses. That one will be a good start."

As Abuela hummed and sliced the vegetables, Victoria knew what she must do. She texted Tyler the address, and one word followed. A word that needed no explanation and would call him to action.

"Help!"

Top of the World

Tyler pounded on the door. The cars were in the driveway, so he knew the Hartwell's were home.

"Please God," he whispered. "Get me to her in time."

Mr. Hartwell cracked it open and said dryly, "Tyler? What's up buddy? The girls are away for the summer."

Tyler tried to hide the panic from his voice. "Can I come in, sir?"

"It isn't a good time. Adoria is on the phone with the treatment center. What is it that you need?"

Tyler hesitated. *Your daughter, safe. With me forever.* "I'd here to ask your permission to visit Victoria at her grandmother's house. I thought we could work on some songs together, maybe find a recording studio in Asheville."

He felt his face blush, and the red patches reached the top of his forehead. He didn't want to worry Mr. Hartwell with Victoria's cry for help, especially with all they had going on. She asked for him and him alone. He couldn't just go without asking her father's permission, or that would set up a guilty conscience. The song part was a stretch, but Mr. Hartwell didn't need all the details.

"You know what? You've always been such a stand-up. Ever thought of getting up on the stage with your own one-man act? Hold on. I'll be right back."

Tyler paced the porch as he waited for Mr. Hartwell's return. When Victoria questioned him about his faith his heart grew heavy with fear. Had she contemplated ending her life? Oh, my God, no. Wouldn't he have seen the signs? They had the teen training at the camp he was a part of last summer. Would he have missed it with his very own best friend?

Please let it not be too late.

"Here you go." Mr. Hartwell returned and handed him a letter. "Make sure you tell her hello when you see her and give her this will you?"

"Thank you, sir. How is Abrianna? Any news?"

He dropped his eyes and bit his lip instead.

"That bad?"

"Have a safe trip, son. You take care of Victoria. I know it will bring her happiness to have you around out there in the sticks. It's a secluded place up there in those hills. Just warning you."

"More time to work on music."

"I bet it will be. Victoria took her songbook. One day the two of you will be famous. I see it all happening for you, traveling all around the world, living a life of adventure. She has a special talent. I just wish she knew how powerful it was."

"I'm working on her," Tyler said.

He shook Mr. Hartwell's hand before he hopped over the rail and headed straight to the VW. He called his parents at work and explained he wanted to see Victoria for the weekend, not to worry, and he would check in with them. He also had to agree that he would sleep in the van. Another uncomfortable promise he would have to keep, but for her and his parent's approval, it would be worth it.

It wouldn't be as if they were headed for trouble if they decided to take off on the summer tour. Maybe when they crossed the North Carolina line, to someplace new, he would open up to her. and tell her the truth.

Tyler mapped all of the spots on the internet and looked for the perfect place that would just jump out at him where he could give her the ring. He'd bought it with his first job from landscaping for the subdivision the summer before, and he carried it around in his pocket for a sign, his Spirit, something, to signal the time. His Mom told him the story about when his Pops gave her a promise ring, and how it was like a sign of purity to stay committed until their wedding day.

This was unheard of in the high school circles he traveled, and he wanted to be the wolf, not follow the sheep. Set trends. The basketball team held him in respect enough because of his jump shot. He didn't care about the stereotype just because he played rock music and wanted to start a band everyone thought he liked to party. And it didn't bother him one bit when people joked him about his Christianity because Jesus was mocked, too. Knowing who he was in Jesus gave him all of the strength he needed to stand up for what was right.

The summer tour stop at Newport News would be the best place to give her a ring. They held the music festival along a beachfront pier, and he thought that would set the perfect backdrop to create a memory for her.

She called out to him for help, so why couldn't he just focus on that instead of his needs or feelings. He refused to turn into a jerk. Tyler could be patient a little longer because he waited years for this. He could wait another couple of months.

Even though Tyler came from a strict family, they were also lenient with what they allowed him to do. Trust and honesty helped build that relationship. His parents were the ones who came up with the idea to take the old tent out of the shed and set it up in the yard for Victoria so she could have a place to go hang out if the pressure got too much in her house.

His Pops showed him the video on how to make a plank swing in the fence and bought him all the hardware to create her a way to their backyard. His Mom helped him secure the summer tour tickets and let him use her credit card with a guarantee that the bill would be paid on time with his Cook's salary. He almost had the payments covered.

And now this.

With the good ol' boy theme song of his life in the background, the fact still remained that he lied for years, to himself, to her. Victoria was and would always be his girl.

Something was not right, and he knew it today. The call shook him to the core. He had witnessed to other youth in the church, in the camp, but never to her. He cared about her salvation, but he didn't want to push her away. *Is that what he had done today? Had he messed up any chance with her? Did this whole ordeal with her sister and parents just drive her over the edge?*

Tyler's thoughts were all over the place and were too busy for the radio. Music would bring him no solace. He redialed her number, and this time she answered.

"Do you need me to call 911?"

"No, I promise. Something has happened here, though. I can't really talk about it on the phone. I just need to see you, and whatever this is about might make some sense. Nothing really seems to fit when you aren't around."

"And that's why I'm coming. You know all you have to do is call, and I'll come running."

"That sounds like an old R & B song."

He sang, "Baby, you know you've got me on the dime. Gotta give you all my time. Nothing gonna take your place. So, hold on, I'm racing to ya. Gonna get to you tonight."

"That's why I need you. For outbursts like these."

"You calling my impromptu lyrical genius an outburst? I take offense. You better go grab your songbook and write that junk down because that's gonna be a hit."

"I need you, Tyler. Please hurry."

"It feels like I'm driving to the top of the world. Just hang tight. I'm on my way, sweet darling."

She needed him. He would be there in two hours and twenty-eight minutes, to be exact. It gave him time for prayers, a rehearsed conversation, maybe even to practice the song to her if the time was right. If he couldn't speak to her about how he felt, he could at least share his lyrics with her. Maybe then she would see they were all about her and have hope. Perhaps then she could believe.

When he heard her voice, it calmed Tyler's nerves a little. *If anything happened to his girl...*

He was a praying man. He had no shame. As tears coursed down his face, he prayed to the One who he knew He could trust. God, I ask you, protect her until I can get to her. Keep her, Lord, in your loving hand. Amen.

****

"That was your mother on the phone," Abuela called through the door.

All the secret talk of exorcisms and skin-walkers made her uneasy about being around Abuela, and she needed her distance. Even the smell of the food made her nauseous. Flashes of the exorcised people free of demons captured in polaroid shots still floated in her mind. Fear was an ugly headed thing. She knew all too well. Maybe she should have stayed at home.

"I can talk to her if she is still on the line," Victoria replied.

"No, it's not that. Can I come in? I think it's best we talk a spell."

Victoria sat up on the bed.

She watched her grandmother amble across to her, years weighed heavy on her frame. She had spiderweb crinkles along the sides of her face, her forehead furrowed in grave concern. Her wrinkles were a beautiful reflection of the life she lived, and even though her appearance had aged dramatically from the portrait framed in the hallway, the intensity of love still lived to soften her facial features. She felt ashamed when she jumped to conclusions, then her thoughts fell to Tyler. She would have to tell her he was on the way. Guilt resurfaced.

Victoria asked, "What did she have to say? It was about Abrianna, wasn't it? Is she gone?"

"You could say that," Abuela said. "Those doctors gave her a label because money demands such lies – Dissociative Identity Disorder."

Victoria questioned, "You don't believe them? You think it's something else, don't you?"

Abuela said, "I'm scared to say without examining her myself. If only your Abuelo were alive. He'd know what to do. He had the gift to see the light and the darkness, a spiritual discernment. With him not here, it will be up to us to figure this whole thing out. But there's no way we can get to her now, and she will have another six more months there."

Victoria said, "That's a long time."

She remembered the short case notes from the journals. The durations were brief, not months. If all of this were true, her sister wouldn't have a chance.

"A long time for the DID to take over her."

"I thought you said it wasn't a mental illness?"

Abuela said, "I don't. My spirit tells me it's the demons of desolation crushing her soul."

"Well, I pray the doctors are right. We should trust the system. What did Mami say?"

Abuela said, "Your mother turned from God many years ago. She will not look to any spiritual warfare, instead accept the automatic trick of the troubled psyche, one she can check out on the web and feel validated by scientific research. I've lived a life of knowing that just as Heaven exists, so does Hell. With that understanding, it brings hope and the wrath of the world to those who inhabit it."

Victoria said, "I want to make all of this just go away."

Abuela answered, "You might be the only one who can."

Victoria frowned. "What do you…"

A horn blew outside. Tyler was still a couple of hours out, and she hadn't had the nerve to tell Abuela she invited him to come without her permission.

Abuela clapped and pulled her hair back as she went to the window to peek out.

Jacoby Wethington had come to visit, bringing his arsenal with him.

With All My Heart

"**W**ell, I'll be a chicken wing," bellowed Jacoby. He grabbed Abuela and spun her to pure giddiness. The lines seemed to fade, and she was back to her youthful sprite self.

"I'd like to introduce you to Manuel Ortega's granddaughter. My Nelita, Victoria Elizabeth Hartwell."

"Victoria?" He held out his hand to her in a grand gesture of a gentleman, "To conquer. Elizabeth. An oath of God. You had that name picked out many years ago, did you not, My Lita, My Love?"

He called her that for the second time. It didn't sit right with Victoria. Maybe the old timer was hitting on her Abuela. Not cool.

Jacoby Wethington was a built, tall man with a slight limp in his left leg. Victoria watched as he ran his hands through his thick hair salted at spots that made him appear like a distinguished professor from a history documentary. His expression carried the softness of a kind man.

He laughed. "Look at her. She is trying to size me up which makes for a keen observer, good quality for the work ahead."

Abuela said, "No bother, Victoria. Father Jacoby will stay awhile. He's harmless, well, to our kind anyway. He is just an old geezer with a fake name."

"Again? Do you have to bring this up now? I liked the name Harry. It suited me, sounded hermit-like, respectable. A name like

Harry is so unassuming. It's not mysterious enough, more like the old chap with a pipe sitting in a parlor chair. I needed plain, so I became Harry."

Victoria asked, "You chose Harry as a fake name?"

"Harry Houdini inspired me to create my alias if you must know."

Victoria said, "Oh, I get it. You wanted to escape like an illusionist."

"Pretty much," he said as he swatted at Abuela and missed. "You see she could still find me."

"You were the last one he called before he…"

As they settled at the dinner table, he reached out and grabbed their hands, then blessed the food. Victoria didn't quite know the drill. Should she repeat the words after him? She held their hands as they sat around the small wooden table. If she wasn't so nervous about Tyler coming without Abuela's permission, or how Harry or Jacoby was looking so intently at her grandmother, she might have noticed the jolt of current that ran through her as they all touched.

Jacoby's voice floated like a shadow hovering over him filled with regret. "Sorry I wasn't here during the time of mourning."

Abuela whispered, "You didn't miss a thing. It's still going on."

"Sorry to hear that, too. To be out of the body is to be present with the Lord."

Abuela threw her fork, the clanking scared them both. "Don't you throw scripture around at me at my dinner table. I know it. I know it well."

"He wouldn't want you to wear this shadow of a life. You aren't wearing black but you might as well be."

"Hold your tongue there, priest. You should wear black and you aren't, so let me question that. I will say this, for every second without Manuel Ortega is every bit of life I live in pain. You should know what that feels like, the heart of someone you love taken from you. Do you still mourn? Do you still grieve? Cry at night when no one is near you? Cry in the sun because he can't see the light of it or feel the warmth of it anymore?"

"I didn't mean to upset you, My Lita, My Love. I was just trying to pay my respects."

Victoria's frazzled nerves sizzled at the talk of death at the table. "Why do you keep calling her that? Can you give that a rest? Call her Adelita. Mrs. Hernandez Ortega for all I care, just not that."

Father Jacoby and Abuela both stared at each other, then burst out laughing. The bellyaching kind of laugh that brings health to those who are sick.

Abuela patted her hand as she wiped the tears. "Calm down, dear. That was my endearing title between the two. That was what Manuel called me, but you wouldn't know that. I guess it became my alias."

"I'm not flirting with your grandmother. I'm a priest, maybe without the collar tonight but I still hold my vows sacred. Father Harry, Father Jacoby, whichever works for you, servant of Christ is more like it. At your beck and call, little lady."

Victoria hung her head, ashamed at her outburst. "Sorry I overreacted. I've done that more than once today."

"You mean since when you were caught snooping in your grandfather's basement?" He pointed to all of the journals stacked on the counter, then took a large mouthful of spaghetti and made little humming noises as he ate.

"Pretty much," confessed Victoria.

Was this like the movies? Had she just openly admitted a sin to a priest, and would he give her so many Hail Mary's to repeat for repentance? She still wasn't sure how all this worked, and to fire direct questions to a man, eating what Victoria still visualized as intestines, might not be appropriate.

"You should have seen the look on her face when I caught her. Precious."

They clinked wine glasses and leaned in close to tell of a time when Manuel would have loved to train up his granddaughters in the way that they should go so they would not depart from it.

"And that brings me to why I called. We have a serious problem. One of our kinds of problems. The Way might need contacting, but until then we need to pray over this situation for insight."

"And what would that problem be?"

Victoria glanced up and saw the lights circle in the front yard, bouncing in the uneven grass like beams on a dance floor. "We might have another one to add to the list."

Abuela let out a frantic squeal. "Why, are you expecting someone? Jacoby, hide!"

Victoria held out her hand to stop him from rising from the table. "I kinda called my best friend Tyler, and he just drove up from Raleigh."

Abuela's hand fluttered over her heart as if the organ itself needed fanning to regain rhythm. "Oh my."

Father Jacoby said, "Why not have another one join the crowd? This is starting out to be one interesting welcome home party."

****

"So, let me get this straight," yelled Abuela. "My own Nieta actually believed that I could harm a single head of hair on her head? What in the world gave you such a wild idea? Please enlighten us, Miss Imagination Station."

Tyler stood on the porch. The moths circled overhead as if he had a halo. The idea of Victoria's first chance at a selfie to see their portrait went right out the window, along with every other plan they had for the summer. Tyler tried to cover his mouth to hide his amusement. What made it worse was that he was smiling, finding this scene a comical one unfolding at her expense.

"You talked about bringing someone back from the dead. I thought you would do some necromancy spell."

"I was talking about Jacoby, or Henry, or whoever he is this week! I was talking about contacting my best friend for half my life, who I hadn't spoken with for ten years, all for you. For Abrianna. To protect my family, silly girl, not cast spells!"

"I see that now, Abuela. Don't be mad." She also saw where her mother inherited her quick temper.

Her Abuela glanced at Jacoby, then at Tyler shuffling his feet and hiding his urge to laugh. After a quick size up, she confirmed, "I know he is of the faith. His glow is a strong one, one of the strongest I've seen in some time."

Jacoby asked, "Do you think they are the next..."

Abuela said, "Time will tell, not you. Not me. So, no more of that talk. I've got to figure out what to do with him now he's here."

Victoria stepped in front of him. "Please forgive me. I panicked. I needed to talk to him about the basement. About Abrianna. Because I knew if anyone could help, maybe he could. It isn't his fault. Can we just please start over?"

Father Jacoby piped in, "Forgiveness bears the fruit of Christian life." He held out his hand and shook Tyler's firmly. "I am Father Jacoby Wethington. You are of the faith, and are welcome here."

Tyler asked, "Of the faith?"

"You know, one of us. The Way, or Jesus Freaks as those who don't understand lovingly refer to us."

He grinned. "Well, sir. I wouldn't quite put it that way. I do love the Lord, if that's what you mean."

Abuela put her arm through his and led him into the house. "Of course, you do, dear. Or you wouldn't have stepped over this threshold and made it without your flesh burning and melting off your body to expose your skeleton."

Father Jacoby frowned. "Don't go there until after I eat, My Lita, my Love. I still have my plate of spaghetti waiting."

Victoria followed in behind them, trying to process the whole scene. Had her grandmother just welcomed Tyler into the home without question? Maybe it was a good thing that Father Jacoby had arrived to soften her defenses.

Tyler glanced behind his shoulder and winked at Victoria. "I'm in like Flynn."

"Flynn, I like that name," replied Father Jacoby. "When this last job is over, I think I'm adopting that one. Henry Flynn. That has a nice ring to it, doesn't it?"

"Last job?" Abuela said, "This might just be the first of many, my dear old friend. There is something in the midst of us that needs to be put in its place."

Father Jacoby said, "Let me guess. Hell has come to Earth in a handbasket."

Victoria added, "And came knocking on our door."

While There is Breath

Tyler tried his best to listen to the story unfold. He was aware of bits and pieces, but not all of the events that occurred in the house right next door. *A demon?* The thought made him shiver. He leaned his head against his knees, and his hair swept the plankboards of the den floor. *Dear Lord, protect and save Abrianna so she may stand against the wiles of the devil.*

Victoria handed him one of her grandfather's journals, and he flipped through it. "It all didn't come together for me until today. There are some things you need to know about my grandfather, and it might be why they've come to attack Abri."

He said, "I'm scared for you."

Victoria asked, "For me?"

Abuela patted her hand, "For your soul, dear. He fears for your soul. You could be next. You might be on to something. Revenge possession. Attacking the Ortega family, going with the weakest, the youngest, and breaking us apart from the ground up."

Father Jacoby sighed, leaned against the couch and pulled out a crucifix from his inside suit pocket. "Are you baptized, Victoria?"

Victoria frowned. "No. My parents didn't believe in any of that stuff."

Father Jacoby looked to Adelita in shock. "What a pity. I know what you and Manuel wanted for your family. You raised Adoria in The Way, and still, she departed from it. There is still hope, and while there is breath, there is hope."

"Adoria blamed God for taking Manuel away from us. You know how much he traveled around the country for his work. We've seen it in the business before when rebellious natures take over. When Manuel passed on, she couldn't understand how he had given his life to the Lord for it to be taken when he was young. But God's ways are his own …"

"And not for our understanding," Father Jacoby finished her sentence. "We need to cleanse your house. We also need to get your sister back."

"But how? She is in Massachusetts, at Cambion Heights."

Father Jacoby sat up straight and said, "Where did you say she was?"

"Up North, some treatment facility for adolescents. It came recommended, and my parents didn't have a choice. They couldn't care for her at home. It was getting worse."

Without a word, he walked out. Abuela ran after him. Their sudden absence rattled Victoria. The night grew more bizarre by the minute. As crazy as it sounded, Victoria could sense something rising within her. A love, a power, a need. *God, I feel the dangers lurking. I believe all of this could be real, that means you must be, too. God, help me. Show me the way.*

Tyler reached for Victoria's hand. "Come here."

Victoria moved from the recliner to sit beside him, and the warmth of him made her just want to curl up in his arms. She leaned her head on his shoulder instead.

"I'm sorry I made you come."

"I'm not. Fighting the devil might not have been on my to-do list today, but then again, Christians must suit up for those attacks, anyway. In all truthfulness, I would fight for you any day of the week."

"Every hour?"

"Of every day."

He picked up the silver crucifix and turned it over in his hands. "There is power in the name of the Lord, not the object. This symbolizes the power of Christ over death and sin."

Victoria said, "I want to know more. I just feel so ignorant about God, and all of this stuff. I feel as if I should know these things, like I was meant to know them. Something is happening, Tyler. I don't understand what it is, my chest is heavy with it. When I held the Bible and read in my Abuelo's study, it was as if my heart was on fire."

"I wish I could tell you everything I have experienced and all I know of God so you would believe. I just don't think it works that way. It's something you have to find on your own. It sounds like you might just get there. You know what that means?"

He caught her chin and tilted her head up. His hand slid to cup her cheek. Her heart was on fire again, but this time it was from the warmth of his hand pressed against her face.

She bit her lip and tried to push back the tears. "What?" *Tell me you love me, and I'll tell you how much you are the breath and hope in me.*

Father Jacoby and Abuela interrupted, carrying bags and a briefcase.

Abuela dropped the ones she was holding down on the rug with a thud and said, "The Arsenal."

He pulled out an electronic device from the bag still strapped on his shoulder and turned it on. It looked more like a prototype for a new gaming system but instead of a console, it was some tracking device. He typed in the treatment facility's address. Father Jacoby held it up for them to see. Tyler stepped forward for a closer look.

Father Jacoby bellowed, "It's just what I feared. When you said the word Cambion, I knew right away what we were dealing with. The word Cambion means child of demons. Good God, My Lita, look at this."

The architectural blueprints of the building teemed with tiny red dots. They moved like an infrared target in real time. There were dozens of them.

Abuela whispered, "Dios Mio. There are so many of them. Look at the shape of the connecting buildings, the design of the pentagram itself speaks of evil. Are we too late? Please, Jacoby, tell me it is not too late."

Father Jacoby prayed, "Turn unto the Lord your God: for he is gracious and merciful, slow to anger, and of great kindness, and repenteth him of the evil."

Victoria said, "I want to understand all of this. I want to know God, too."

She felt Tyler's hand rest against her arm, and could've sworn she heard his heartbeat, it thudded so.

Abuela said, "Child. Your God knows you. To start, you need to believe. It might sound simple just to say to you believe but that's how simple it is. Conversion is not some fancy show but an opening up of your heart to replace the stone with the love of Christ. Believe He is. Faith will carry you through those times when you aren't so sure."

Father Jacoby stepped forward and took Victoria by the hands.

"Come, my child. Let's go for a walk and talk, shall we?"

Victoria stepped in closer to Tyler. "Will you pray for me?"

Tyler said, "Yes." His voice grew to a soft whisper against her hair. "Always."

****

Tyler watched as the love of his life headed for the front door with Father Jacoby. He wanted to go with them, to witness to her, to be the one that led her to Christ.

Abuela grabbed his shoulder. "That leaves the two of us. We've got some business to attend to ourselves. I have to show you something. Something that will change the course of your life."

Tyler followed Adelita through the hallway and into the study. He felt her weaken with each step and recognized how much this took its toll on her. He escorted her until they made it to the steps that led down into the abyss.

"Wow."

"Is that what you think, now?" Abuela waved her arm. "Take a look but be careful not to touch anything that's not a holy object."

Tyler scanned the cramped room filled with trinkets, statues, and crosses at every turn. Bookcases were lined against the walls with ancient texts. Oh, how he would like to get his hands on those. What caught his attention more than anything was the significant number of crucifixes of every shape, color, and size lining the walls.

"Why so many crosses on the walls?"

Abuela said, "For every possession Manuel exorcized. For every family he helped, he kept the cross he used to call out the demon and cast it back to hell."

"And these, so many unused." He lifted the holy water bottles and wondered if there would still be the strong hint of soda mixed in with the blessed water.

"Manuel had so much work to do but the Lord felt otherwise. The truth we both know remains. There are many mansions in Heaven, and I believe that not only the Lord is saving a place for me, but Manuel will be there to welcome me to my true home. This place is just a temporary stay, and my permanent residence will be mighty fine. Mighty fine indeed."

"True."

"Truth is, there is something about you, Tyler. I needed you down here to see it. I feel Manuel's presence in his workshop more than any other room in the house." Her eyes grew misty as she held a portrait of her and Manuel. "Two times in one day and I haven't been down here in ten years." She held up a picture and said, "Who would've thought we'd find our way back to this again, mi amor?"

Tyler asked, "What are you looking for?"

"I'm looking for the ones to carry on his work. Our work. Manuel and I were a team. He did the heavy lifting, I guess you could call it. I was the prayer warrior. I sense the strength and maturity of the faith you possess. You are full of the Spirit of the Lord."

He grinned. "You could say that. Through grace, I've been saved through faith if that is what you mean."

She stepped in closer and eyed him. "There it was again. I have to ask you this, and with all seriousness answer me. What is your calling, your gift?"

"Not sure yet, about that part anyway. I figure I'm too young to have the gift of the Spirit given to me."

"Hogwash. You just haven't been put in the proper situation yet to experience it, that is what I'm figuring. You have one. All Christians do because Jesus said it would be."

"Even Victoria?"

"Even Victoria. In fact, I have an inkling to believe Victoria will be the next Manuel in the family."

"What do you mean by that?"

"Manuel was what his grandfather was before him. She will be an exorcist, whether she likes it or not. It is what will be and denying a calling from the Lord only gets you swallowed up by whales."

Doubt rose in Tyler's voice, "I was just praying she would see the light, not cast demons into pigs."

"The light will bring Abrianna home to us. And so will your prayers."

Tyler answered, "Victoria is out there now receiving the Gospel of Christ. I have proof that the fervent prayer of a righteous man availeth much."

She smiled. "I knew it. We can go up now. Come on, my little-kindred spirit. Wait til I tell Jacoby."

"Tell him what?"

"Your gift child and what that means for your future."

He frowned. "Well, let me in on the secret. I think I deserve to be the first to know."

Abuela closed up the hatch and led him back to where Victoria and Father Jacoby waited for them on the porch. He could tell that Victoria had been crying and recognized tears of redemption because he'd been to the altar praying and laying hands on the people a time or two.

Father Jacoby said, "Neither is there salvation in any other: for there is no other name under heaven given among men, whereby we must be saved."

Abuela said, "And we've got the next step, her baptism."

Victoria stepped forward to face Tyler. "I want Tyler to baptize me."

Abuela smiled and said, "Manuel baptized me, too. How appropriate. That confirms my vision even more."

Tyler held out his arm and asked, "Do you have a water hose? I could spray her! How about a river, a pond? I could dunk her. The bathtub works, too."

Abuela said, "There is a stream right behind the cabin, a good a place as any. Let's all walk down and they can hear our news at the same time."

"Something else happened we need to know about other than this miraculous coming to the saving knowledge of Jesus Christ by our dear sweet, child Victoria?"

"Yeah, Tyler here, this fine young man, he is me. Tyler is Adelita Hernandez Ortega."

Victoria asked, "What's that supposed to mean?"

Father Jacoby laughed. "Don't you get it. Tyler will be your Adelita, and you will be his Manuel."

Victoria smirked. "I think both of you are so old you lost your rockers."

Tyler said, "She means you will be an exorcist, and apparently I will be your Bible quoting, praying sidekick."

Abuela clapped. "Exactly! Now, come along. We have work to do."

Father Jacoby said, "It's time we call on some old friends. It takes a village to fight the forces of darkness, right?"

Victoria said, "I thought it was to raise a child?"

"To kill off a demon horde will take the lot of us and The Way must be called on again."

Tyler asked, "The way? Are you referring to the way, the truth, and the life verse in the Bible?"

Abuela swept up Victoria's hair and roped it in a bun like a crown upon her head. She removed some of her own clips and clasped the loose curls.

"You will find out soon enough. Let's get to the business at hand, and very mighty business indeed. It's Biblical that after one received Christ as the Savior someone baptized them, many of them with their whole family. There wasn't a waiting period, just the act of professing the faith in front of witnesses once they accepted the Lord. Those were dangerous times, where faith was tested and many lost their lives because of it."

Victoria's thoughts conjured up the image of her sister-girl. "Sounds a little like our time."

Tyler slipped off his boots, rolled up his jeans, and waded into the water. He yelped, "Ew-we. This is some cold stepping."

Jacoby said, "Good it's you then, boy. It wouldn't be good for my arthritis."

Victoria followed Tyler. "I wouldn't have it any other way."

Tyler asked her softly, his voice soothing over her nerves and emotions like a sweet balm, "Do you believe in Jesus Christ? Do you believe in the Father, the Son, and the Holy Spirit? Do you believe Jesus rose from the dead and was resurrected to sit at the right hand of the father?"

"I do."

"Then, by the power of the Holy Spirit, I baptize you in water, in truth, and in life you pledge to follow the way of the Lord as long as you live until eternity in heaven."

Abuela wiped tears and shouted. "Amen!"

Victoria came up out of the water, wiped her eyes and felt the joy of the Lord overflowing. That was real. She knew with all of her heart that her life changed at that moment. That very moment she was new.

Tyler put his arms around her, soaked through. "You are my girl, you know."

"I know." Victoria whispered. "Thank you, Tyler."

"Thank Jesus," he replied. "I'm just glad He chose me to stand beside you, no matter what we face.

Father Jacoby said, "I hate to break this up, but let's get you both dried off. We can start our first lesson."

"Tonight? Now," asked Victoria. She watched as the sun traveled down to visit the others awaiting a new day.

"Now," said Abuela. "Dangerous times, remember."

"Yes. Dangerous times indeed."

Speak to Me

E very technological paranormal advancement over the past decade littered the living room. Father Jacoby was more than just a run-of-the-mill priest. He had a plethora of gadgets and manuals of the supernatural kind. Some equipment looked like conventional items scattered at Victoria and Tyler's feet. There were night vision goggles, virtual reality sets, video recorders, gaming handheld systems, and a stuffed bear. Abuela and Father Jacoby pilfered through the objects and took turns answering the firing barrage of questions directed at every gadget.

"What's this one for?" Tyler asked for the umpteenth time, as he opened up the last camouflage bag.

"I haven't been able to test it yet, which on the grand scheme of life, that means no demons have passed my way to challenge me. It's like an advanced EVP digital recorder, but it transcribes the languages in real time for a better understanding of what we might deal with across cultures and continents. Demons and ghosts don't just come to us with English, Tyler. They like to mix it up a bit, and this might just give me an edge of catching a name they haphazardly throw out thinking they have outsmarted me. I've had so many iterations of this one design, but I think with the help of an old friend I've nailed it with this prototype."

"The name," Victoria said. "I saw that at the end of every anecdotal record that Abuelo kept. Why is that so important?"

Abuela said, "Faith in Christ and the power to cast out demons is the most critical component of a successful exorcism, but knowing the name is like a bait on the hook that catches the fish, latching on to the very core of the beast and reels it out of the soul to cast it back to hell."

Tyler grinned. "That makes me want to go fishing. I got an itch to catch a big one. I bet there are some sweet honey holes around in these parts. Not demons though, bass."

Father Jacoby warned. "Yeah, don't get too eager to step into this struggle for souls. It is a life with evil at every turn. The demons speak, they have a network of communication, their own wifi, so to speak. Devils try to tempt us with unthinkable tricks. They want to steal our joy, our peace, wreck our life if we allow it. We must be strong in the midst of them or one weakness can take us over and drive us over the edge."

Abuela said, "Behold I send you out as sheep in the midst of wolves."

Victoria held up the bulky ghost box amp in her lap and asked, "Can you teach me how to use this equipment?"

Tyler said, "Me, too. I won't let Victoria do this alone. I am supposed to be Abuela, right?"

"Okay, you don't have to keep reminding me of that reference. It's a little weird," admonished Victoria. "How about you just pray for me from the comforts of your own home?"

He pointed her finger at her and said, "Not a chance, sweet thing. I'm with you for the long haul, and you have no other choice but to put up with me."

"But if Abuela says this is dangerous for me, then that means you could also be in the line of fire. I won't have you near any of this if it means you could get hurt."

Father Jacoby said, "Where two or three are gathered in my name, Tyler, do you know that scripture?"

He finished, "So, I will be there also."

"Then, Victoria, you must understand this very truth and accept it. You can never conduct an exorcism alone. If Abuela and I are right, then you and Tyler are more than you realize. Anyway, you can't fight a demon without an assistant or a prayer warrior. I'll train you, that is for sure, and Tyler, too, but I'll do this my way – the right way or not at all."

Victoria felt Tyler's hand cover hers. She said, "We need to do this, even if it's just for Abri."

"No better time than the present, grab the gear and let's take a midnight stroll." Abuela stood up and headed to the cabinet in the kitchen. She grabbed flashlights and her lantern, then moved out to the porch.

Tyler asked, "Right now?"

Father Jacoby laughed. "What about how ready you were earlier to go fishing?"

"Well, that might have been a little presumptuous of me."

Victoria pulled on his hand, lifting him up off the couch. "Let's go, assistant."

"Wait a dog-on minute. I think we need to think of a new title. Tyler the Tough Guy, or Tyler the Tenacious, something along those lines."

She pulled him along. "You don't seem too tough right now. Are you shaking?"

"Yep, right down to my snake boots."

When they walked to the edge of the land, where the earth seemed to stop and become swallowed up with forests, Abuela turned to Father Jacoby before stepping over the invisible line of no return. "Are you sure she is ready? Spiritually, I mean?"

"There is only one way to find out."

With that being said, he pulled out the EVP prototype and secured his pair of goggles. He handed over what looked like a prayer shawl to Abuela, and she draped it over her shoulders. Father Jacoby placed the crucifix in Victoria's hand, the one she brought up from her Abuelo's study.

Tyler asked, "What about me? Do I get a recorder, a tracker, something? I really want to try those night vision goggles, for real." His voice sounded as tense as bungee cords tied around a heavy load of a truck, close to popping loose.

Abuela squeezed his arm for reassurance. "You've got the Word, and that's all you need. The greatest weapon formed against it shall not prosper."

He sighed. "But what if I forget?"

She shrugged. "That is up to you."

Father Jacoby warned. "It's about controlling your emotions and keeping the faith in front of you, not the entity. The entity will see the light and either want to navigate toward it or destroy it. The best advice I ever learned from my mentor, 'Step outside of yourself and let the Spirit take charge.' And that is what I tell you both now. The Holy Spirit is as powerful today as when Jesus was raised from the dead, and it lives in you. The Lord is with you both."

Victoria asked, "So, we can have the out-of-body experience while we conjure up those out of the body or in need of one to steal?"

"Good way of looking at it, except we do not conjure. We only recognize what is present, already there. Then, we give it peace to continue its journey on. Whether it meets light or darkness, that's the judgment and will of God to decide from the life choices they made."

Abuela said, "We never leave a spirit lost because those of us that are of The Way know that there is no greater joy than going home. Many just wander confused and don't even know they are dead. Some leave, others still want to hold on to this world. Either way, we offer them a ticket to the light and serve as a train conductor."

A half-mile in, Abuela stopped their descent from venturing further under the pines. She sat down her lantern on a fallen log and hands raised in praise. Father Jacoby stood still, holding tight to his equipment.

As confident as he appeared, he had to admit he was a little rusty. "It's been ten years for me, too, My Lita, My Love. Can we think about taking this a little slower?"

"Together We Stand Like Pine Trees In A Forest" 2/4 Emmaline At M'pandfield

She did not stop her singing of an old gospel hymn, only swayed back and forth humming how she loved Jesus because He first loved her. Victoria watched as the reader detected motion. Something was coming. Their presence had created a stir.

Her pulse quickened at the sight, and the dot appeared closer now. An orb, moving as if dodging and finding a path, ducked and weaved between thick branches of the pines. She reached out and felt the bark in her palm. *This is real*, she thought. *I can touch this.* But that circle on the screen, it was once real, too. And it was about two feet from her.

Tyler could not see the screen from where he was standing with Abuela. He said, "I think I might be a little dizzy headed?"

Abuela stopped to stare at him, her eyes glinting in the dark. "Then, you sing. Lightheadedness is a sign that an entity could be near because it may want to feast on your energy. Praise is an excellent spirit blocker if the entity is dark."

Tyler prayed aloud, "God give me the words."

Instead of choosing the song he wrote for Victoria or a song from Mark McKinney & Co. on his playlist, another form of worship built within him. He let out first the soft hum, then the solo rose from him without fear or restraint. He sang for his Lumbee people, even though the choral response wasn't echoing around him as he showed me in videos from Homecomings under a tent-circle. Tyler still sang as if he were standing in the drum circle of his cousins back home, the powwow beat resonated for only him to hear in his head, the vocals took a melancholy shape.

Father Jacoby gasped as the first reading appeared on his screen, the words sounding robotic but legible. He held up the screen to Victoria, and she read the words again, "Siyo – Hello – Cherokee Origin."

He said, "It works! I knew it would! And we didn't even have to speak to the spirit first, he found us. Thank you, Jesus, for the insight and the knowledge to build it. Amen."

Abuela asked, "We know you are here. Who are you?"

Tyler lowered his voice, but he did not stop the chanting. He had called a Native American spirit and welcomed it into their circle, and he would not let it feel abandoned now.

"Dagwado Gawonni – My name is Gawonni – Cherokee Origin."

Victoria asked, "Are you at peace here? Do you need help?"

"Alisdelvdi! – Help! – Cherokee Origin."

Abuela commanded, "Are you an evil spirit come to harm us?

"Vtla – No – Cherokee Origin."

Father Jacoby asked, "What happened to you? Why are you here?"

No reply. Abuela set up the speaker box. She asked them all to be silent. Tyler closed down his song, and she urged Victoria to separate from them and stand closer to the box. "You ask him the questions now."

Father Jacoby said, "His name in Cherokee means, He Who Talks. He even converses in the spirit realm. That will be me one day."

Abuela said, "So right, you never shut up. Now let her do her thing. Let's see if she can communicate with him and set his spirit free toward the light."

Victoria stepped forward. "What happened to you? Speak to me. I mean you no harm. I only want to help you, and I promise you I will try to do just that. Speak to me."

The static of the box was so distracting, the sound of the white noise like sandpaper scraping their ears. The FM radio frequency scanned the airwaves and swept for anything that the Spirit could use to communicate.

"Do you speak any English?"

"Some."

Tyler repeated, "He said some. I heard it."

Victoria asked again, "What happened to you?"

"I don't know. Where am I?"

Victoria held herself perfectly still. She felt as if she would take one step to the right or the left, shift her feet, she would disturb the place where the Spirit roamed. He felt so close that her skin prickled.

"Are you lost?"

"Yes."

She turned to Abuela, "How far is the Cherokee Nation from here?"

"About forty miles up the road?"

"Do you want to find your way back home?"

"To Ahyoka."

"Is that a place?"

No response. She tried again, and this time she thought she saw an orb of light travel between the trees. "Is that a woman? Your woman?"

"Yes."

"If you go to your village and she is not there, how will you find her? What if she is in the light? She could have traveled on."

"My people."

Father Jacoby said, "Send him to them. That is his wish. He's s still attached to this world."

Victoria prayed aloud, "God help me guide this poor soul back to his people, to Ahyoka, to the light. Let him go in peace."

Tyler said, "Go East. Go in peace."

The Spirit's last word was, "Ahyoka."

Father Jacoby spoke, "Now, we shall pray for you our Christian prayers. Lead us in the Lord's prayer, Victoria."

Victoria felt nauseous. *What was that?*

Father Jacoby put down the spirit recorder and handed over the Bible to Victoria. As soon as he handed it to her, he realized his mistake. She would not be able to find the verses even if he told her the book. He took it back, turned it to Matthew 6:9-13 and handed it over to her.

Victoria read it aloud. As she did, Tyler's recited it with her. The surroundings were too still, almost too quiet. There were no sounds in the forest, the usual colorful night songs of the cicadas and katydids in harmony were absent. It was as if they, too, recognized the reverence given to the Most High God and took a moment to pray.

When the night started up again, Father Jacoby turned off the equipment and packed up. He took the cross from Victoria and patted her on the arm. "Well, missy. I think you have a gift. You can talk to the Spirits and led them on their way."

Abuela said, "Jacoby, it was mighty fine. I could feel the power of the moving on myself, such a peaceful transition to that it filled my heart with a love that only lets me believe he found exactly what or who he was looking for. Check the sensors."

"No need. You're right about moving on. A second orb appeared to what I could imagine might have been his woman.

By calling her name, he could have found who he was seeking. It wasn't his tribe. He was searching for his lady."

Tyler said, "I can understand that completely."

Father Jacoby said, "What we weren't right about was Victoria. I know she wants to save her sister, but I'm not sure she is the one that can do the job. Lost spirits and vengeful spirits are two separate entities, a walk in the park versus a battle raging against good and evil."

Victoria wanted to disagree. She wanted to shout out he had no faith in her, that she just came face to face with a ghost and didn't cower in fear or run away but she knew he was right. *How could she take the lead when she didn't know which way to turn?*

Tyler said, "I know what your fear is, Father Jacoby, and I think there's a resolution to this problem."

When they made it back to the cabin, Victoria didn't want to go inside. She held on to the porch railing, needing her time alone. "Father Jacoby, I'm sorry I let you down."

He said, "That's not it, dear. If you are talking about not knowing the Lord's prayer, that wouldn't let me down. It would just show me that you are not as equipped as some of us in The Way. You need more time."

Abuela said, "But time is what we don't have, Jacoby, and you know it. We have to make do with what we have, and we have a better shot at facing this demon and saving Abrianna's soul when we gather The Way with us."

"Who said anything about me going with her? With you? I'm here to assess the situation, maybe to train her, but I say in my humble opinion that the girl is not ready to face an evil that eats away life and soul. And me? Not my job anymore. I'm retired."

Tyler interjected. "I know what can make her ready. She needs to read the instruction manual."

Victoria doubted there was such a book. "A guide to all things exorcism actually exists."

Abuela answered, "He means the Bible, dear. You need to read the Bible. How fast of a reader are you?"

She thought of how she stayed up all night reading the *Harry Potter* series, and she did the same with *Twilight*. But she had never owned a Bible before and only held one in her hands the first time that very morning.

"As fast as I need to be," she answered. She shook off the doubt that wanted to push at every corner of her being. "Can I have Abuelo's or is that too much to ask?

Her grandmother returned with Abuelo's Bible that she placed on the lampstand. "It is yours. Now follow all the precepts in it and let the Word be the lamp unto your feet..."

Tyler added, "And the light into your path."

"What am I going to do with you and Jacoby? Both of you like to finish my sentences. You braggarts."

Victoria looked at Tyler. "Will you teach me?"

"Every hour of every day, for as long as it takes."

He grabbed the lantern from Abuela and swung it back and forth as he headed to the porch swing. "It won't be the first time we pulled an all-nighter, and I'm sure it won't be the last."

Father Jacoby advised, "Stick with the New Testament, Tyler. She gets Jesus, she gets it all."

"Agreed. Enough faith to move a mountain, or a demon back to hell, whichever needs to be cast aside first."

"Amen to that," answered Abuela. "Now, come on Father Jacoby. Let's leave the lovebirds to their reading assignment."

Victoria said, "Abuela! I told you we were best friends."

She rolled her eyes and swatted at them both. "Whatever, dear. Just like the time your Abuelo convinced himself that he could fly, full well knowing he could not and broke his arm at seven skydiving off his rooftop in San Juan. We can lie to ourselves all day long, or we can be truthful but lying never got anybody anywhere except with their pants on fire, and that truth shall set you…"

"Free," said Father Jacoby.

"Now, stop that! It's getting annoying, you old coon. Come in here and be useful. Set us on a pot of coffee. Looks like it will be a long night."

"You need to stop embarrassing these youngsters. This kind of night that brings those closer to the light marks the best nights for revelations if you ask me."

"Well, I didn't ask you. I told you to make the Café Pilon."

He winked at Tyler and Victoria then tipped his hat to them, saying, "Carry on," in his Harry, British accent.

Tyler sat the lantern in between them on the swing as he opened the Bible to the Gospel According to Mark, the easiest place he knew to start. He could not speak the words he wanted to say, like how much it overjoyed him at her being saved today, or how terrified he was in the forest when he heard the language of the Cherokee clearly through the recorder. It rattled and confirmed his beliefs at the same time. Tyler could not share how much he so wanted to be her lovebird, to confess just how much he adored her.

Instead, he fell to his comfort and read. Victoria leaned her head against his shoulder, pushing the lantern against them, but he didn't care. She would one day be his, he had no reservations anymore. If he had to rid the entire world of demons to be by her side, that would be just what he would do. For the rest of his life.

"The beginning of the gospel of Jesus Christ, the Son of God; As it is written in the prophets, Behold, I send my messenger before thy face, which shall prepare thy way before thee..."

Just Beneath the Surface

Tyler closed the Bible, stretched and rocked them sideways in the swing. Victoria almost lost her balance, but he positioned her back up. "Another bucket list crossed off for me."

"We've seen the sunrise before, Tyler, like when we were thirteen."

"No, silly. Reading the Bible with you."

"More along the lines of reading the Bible to me. I wasn't much help, was I?"

"You were perfect."

"Far from it. Did I ask enough questions?"

He laughed. "Without the help of the old internet here, we might still be on John 1."

"That was my favorite Gospel of the New Testament."

"Why?"

"It just felt like he had a special in, somehow. He spoke in a proper way that just rested well in my soul. I liked it. I know that doesn't sound scholarly or have a literary analysis ring to it like Mrs. Altman would want us to answer in English class."

"One of my favorite books of the Bible has to be Ephesians. The whole putting on the whole armor of God makes me feel all manly, ready to go fight a war."

"I want to read the rest."

Abuela interrupted them. "One day, you will. The words of our Lord and Savior need to swim awhile in your soul."

"Now I get why you have that verse beside my bed in the spare room."

"I prepared that for your visit."

Father Jacoby came out a long robe and fluffy slippers. "Were you stirring up trouble before she even got here?"

Abuela said, "I had an intuition that something wasn't right with the world. Adoria was so short with me about Abrianna. I've prayed for a miracle."

"Miracles happen." Tyler squeezed Victoria's hand. "Sleep does wonders, too. I need me some shut eye."

Father Jacoby said, "You get some rest yourself, Victoria. We'll do more ghost hunting later."

"Why ghosts? I thought I had to go up against demons, not capture voices on a box."

"Let's put it this way. If you can withstand the jump scare when you realize that something real is on the other side, it helps strengthen your resolve. When you can communicate with the dead, and speak to the Spirits that long for the light without fear, then you may be a tenth ready to face an evil that can rise against you to manipulate and harm you. You need training. You need time. Maybe a year or two."

Victoria said, "You can train me. You can come with me. Abuela, too. We can go as a team. But a year with Abri like that, you are wrong. I saw her. You didn't. Believe me when I tell you she is no longer Abri."

Abuela said, "I apologize for not coming to you. If only I would have known. Jacoby, she is right. A year is out of the question. Let them rest. Let's go out once more and build her up. But it has to be soon."

Father Jacoby sighed. "There is more at work here than snatching Abrianna's soul. It's a part of a greater plan, something brewing beneath the surface that is toying with us."

Tyler stood up and yawned. "I'll be there with you to see Abri safe and Victoria unharmed, but first if I don't get some sleep, I'll be no good to anyone."

He hopped down off the porch.

"Where's your strapping, handsome Lumbee boy going? Looks like the wrong way. We do have a couch."

"I can't, sorry. I promised my people I'd sleep in the van. Speaking of, we need a wrapped sign. I knew this old classic would be useful. I've got to draw us out a logo."

Father Jacoby asked, "Where did you find this miscreant?"

Victoria watched him yank on the sliding door of the van, begging it to open as if it heard his commands. "Blame it on the Holy Angels daycare teacher. She put us both in time out for drawing on the walls. He became my sidekick way back when."

Abuela said, "Well isn't that a story to tell the grandchildren. Go rest now. I'll wake you up in five hours. We will spend the rest of the day in training, and I have just the plan to catapult us to the next level."

Father Jacoby raised his eyebrows. "And what would that be?"

"Daylight is wasting. No more talking. I need some prayer time."

Father Jacoby pointed toward Tyler and said, "That's a stand-up boy right there. Don't find many of integrity these days, young or old. He's a keeper."

Victoria thought, I know that, and I plan on keeping him forever.

****

Silas Amon knew that the time drew near. His body felt the energy pulsating like the fire in his veins. His bones ached with it.

The body he wore smelled of mothballs, like a cheap overcoat with a button missing, a tear here or there. Past the welcome, he stayed too long in the body during the initial stages of the plan, decades in the making to rise Cambion to the level to accept him as a leader in the community. Silas' reward after years of searching was so close, he could taste the victory on his forked tongue.

The form was not as spry as it once was, and the smallest inclination of rain made his joints throb around the knees. His eyesight grew dim. What was this age of man that broke apart piece by piece? His soul combusted with an eternal flame of destruction and burned the body slowly from the inside out. He may need to find another host soon, one that could withstand the transition for just a little while longer.

"None of these will do," he said, as he roamed the halls checking in on the patients and flipped through images on online dark sites that offered bodies for demons. Yes, those existed. The dark web became a mysterious playground for evil to thrive.

A nurse was being brutalized by a demon boy, eyes dilated black, and stared her down into submission. Oh, the pleasure of youth. Silas watched through the glass. It was necessary the patients kept their health, and feeding or keeping the demon children hydrated was no easy task when they would occasionally rise to challenge the positional authority of the assigned caregiver. *Rebellious punks*, he thought, then smiled at the irony. Demons would be demons, after all.

"It is speaking," he heard the discussion in room seven through the closed door.

His energy channeled to that spot by a connection gift bestowed from the Master. No other in Cambion possessed the level of his powers, and they never would. Well, he would have to give that away soon, but Silas was well aware of his purpose and what the union of his power to the host would kindle. Soon enough.

"He speaks, you say." Dr. Silas Amon entered the room.

A nurse slid across the wall and found her nearest corner. Another leaned in closer, holding on to the arm rails. Should he warn her? Nah, he enjoyed the show.

"It said something strange, I didn't understand it."

"I record everything in this room so I shall decipher. Move you imbecile. Leave us."

Dr. Amon made a fast, professional decision that would be effective at once without question. He reassigned his lead nurse to care for him. When she arrived, he advised her of the care plan. Her pleasure at such an honor to serve him was clear by the look of pride across her face. She leaned in to ask how she could show her gratitude.

"By doing your job," Silas Amon said as he pushed her aside. "Now, let me watch the video surveillance. *He* spoke."

Silas didn't need to rewind the recording much to see the jerking movements of the two nurses in the room that showed *his* voice startled them, frightened them more like it. He adjusted the volume so he could take in the full force of the evil guttural sound from the depths of the belly was so thrilling to take in as a sweet elixir to bring on all ills. Oh, how it must have unnerved the humans when they first heard the demons speak among them. Wait, oh wait, until they listen to *him*. It will bring back the ancients, the time of old when fire ruled in pestilence. When they thought supernatural forces spawned Black Death. This death of days was arriving and he could faintly hear the knocking of it from the gates of hell.

The time to reign was near, no denying it. Supernatural forces would be at work against science and forward thinking, progress and technology. The rise of the prophets and demonic legions would destroy all that and the fields would lay desolate.

Silas Amon's dog-teeth smile spread across his face when he heard him speak, "Gather ye together first the tares, gather the tares for me. Bind them in bundles to burn them, burn them all for me."

Yes, yes, yes, yes, burn them, burn them, burn them all, we shall. And we will bind them one by one and burn them all for thee.

Two by Two

The Landslide Coffee Shop didn't seem to be the place where Victoria imagined she would take her exorcism training to the next level. She could use a vanilla latte, so she held her tongue out of her love for coffee house smells and good vibes.

A makeshift stage was crammed in the corner, with a cheap black tarp as a backdrop signifying the performance area. Victoria knew right away that as she craved the latte, Tyler yearned for the stage as he headed over in that direction, holding up his phone for a selfie she was sure he would snap out to his cousins back home. They dreamed of starting up their own band one day and hitting the road in the van. She could be his lead singer, but those were dreams for another day.

She left the line and grabbed his arm, pulling herself closer to him, their cheeks touching. "Humor me."

Tyler raised his phone high, extending it for the perfect angle and snapped. "I'll share it to your story."

She couldn't breathe, let alone answer him. His fresh stubble tickled against her soft skin. God, let me have him. She didn't need to see if the love glowed brightly between them as it did for her grandparents. In her secret place, where more than just her lifeline swelled, she knew that it beat solely for him.

Abuela broke her trance. "Order up, lovebirds. Get in line. The sisters will be here any minute, and we'll hit the road."

Father Jacoby grinned. "Oh, the sisters are still kicking it, huh? I figured they were about two steps in the grave when I left this place behind."

Tyler questioned, "Wouldn't two steps in be already fully in? I thought the saying was one foot in the grave?"

"You'll see what I mean when the old folks come to town. Standing beside them will at least make me look debonair and Clark Gableish."

Abuela said, "So, is that the look you are going for these days with the Panama hat, Harry?"

"What? Come on. It has to be better than my 80s hair band phase."

That caught Tyler's attention. "You, with the eyeliner and teased up hair? You play, Father?"

"Yes, sir I do. I play the guitar. Chasing ghosts stopped me from chasing dreams."

"Don't blame it on no ghosts," Abuela chided. "The church would not allow one of their parish priests to go running up and down the highways with groupies for miles on end. You had responsibilities to the parish, that is what priestly sacrifice is. The one thing that you wish you had you must give up you did for the love of Christ and the church, right? Isn't that in your vows somewhere?"

"For many priests that meant family relationships and a lifetime of serving the church, but for me that meant touring with the big hair bands."

Tyler sang a chorus of a power ballad. Heads turned but smiled when the shock wore off and amusement crossed the patrons' faces at the recognition he could actually sing.

As soon as they all had their coffees in hand, Abuela pointed out toward the street. "See, don't they look dead already? There they are now. Wouldn't you know they had to make a grand entrance?"

Victoria said, "Abuela, sometimes the things you say!"

Father Jacoby replied, "She has been confessing over that mouth of hers for years. I should know."

What had to be two of the oldest living women in America, shimmied out of a red Lamborghini, grasping crystal topped canes in their hands as they hobbled their way inside. Their voices rose over the music, one cackled at the other's joke.

"It's Jacoby, come to town! Wait 'til Solomon St. Pierre hears of this."

"Look at him," the other said as she elbowed her sister, "Still sexy as ever. I always said the angels cried for me in Heaven when you said you put on that black robe. Haven't you ever heard what the Father doesn't know, won't hurt him."

Abuela scowled and said, "And there is no creature hidden from His sight, but all things are open and laid bare to the eyes of Him with whom we have to do."

Father Jacoby mumbled for Victoria and Tyler to hear. "See how Bible verses save."

Victoria smiled. "Amen."

Tyler said, "You are getting the hang of this."

Betty Lou said, "So, why did you call us with such an urgency that required us to leave the house without makeup?"

"Sisters, I would like to introduce you to my granddaughter, Victoria Elizabeth Hartwell, and her friend, Tyler Locklear."

The shorter of the two said with a sophisticated air, "I'm Dorothy Lamar, and this is my sister, Betty Lou St. Pierre.

Victoria was careful with the weight of her handshake because she felt she would shatter them like glass. "It's nice to meet you."

"Oh, my." whispered Dorothy. Her eyes widened, and the full effect of surprise washed over her. "You are Manuel's granddaughter. You have his gift. I see the aura of the light with her, Adelita. It doesn't feel as strong as Manuel's, but it has time to grow with spiritual formation."

Abuela nodded in approval and said, "And that's where you come in."

Betty Lou said, "You require our services again, huh? After the last time, I would have thought you would have had no more meetings with us. Seeing his Spirit come back to haunt put it out of you."

Abuela shooed them off. "It was a comfort, more than you know. Just startled me and caught me off guard."

Dorothy Lamar asked, "What's really going on here? I sense an earnestness about her that is unsettling."

Victoria leaned in closer, "It's my sister. She has some type of affliction, and I have to rescue her."

Dorothy and Betty Lou locked gazes.

Betty Lou said, "A demon with your sister, you say. Then, we have just the job for that. Sisters have to stick together after all. Look at the two of us, joined at the hip in the two-by-two since we were called to be ASPs."

"He sent them out two by two." Tyler understood now. "Do you all go out in twos?"

Abuela said, "It is biblical, now isn't it? Jesus sent them out two by two to cast out demons. We can't go against the Word. That's when we start blending in with the world and there isn't any compromising where we're going."

Victoria said, "If you don't mind all the questions, what are ASPS?"

Betty Lou answered, "Academy of Spiritual Paranormal Studies. It's our official title, and you can go check out our website. Solomon came up with it." She winked. "Solomon's my mighty-fine husband, who actually is a genius. He keeps up our appearance schedule, lectures, the website, and all our social media accounts, not to mention he is our techie."

"Tell your husband, the genius, that the parts he shipped were just what I needed for the newest project I've been working on."

Betty Lou thanked Father Jacoby. "So, you were the one that has been contacting him lately. I knew he was up to something. He got that light back in his eyes and that spring in his old step. Giving him a project to keep his hands busy has been good for his soul. You know that idle hands are the devil's workshop, they say, and the older we get we can suffer a time or two from the lack of the activity we had in the old days."

Dorothy asked, "So, saving your sister calls for some training. I'm figuring she looks mighty young for the job. And you, are you supposed to be her two-by-two?" She looked at Tyler.

"Yes, mam, I am proud to say I am."

Abuela said, "Training in progress. We've had our first contact with the Spirit realm, but it was in a safe environment."

Victoria exhaled. "You say safe, like in the middle of the forest, pitch black, in the dead of night – talking to a Cherokee that was long departed, a safe environment?"

"Of course," answered Abuela, "And surrounded by seasoned veterans. Nothing could have happened to you there as long as we were present, and I'm sure somewhere in your subconscious you knew that."

"I know you won't let anything harm me," Victoria said, "But I don't think anything about this line of work feels safe."

Father Jacoby turned serious. "Then, you are farther along than I expected. In my estimation, most youngsters today would get the thrill of the ghost hunt, the gadgets like they are starting on some reality television show. This is no made for TV special and no adventure. There is a soul trapped, whether it is meant to do evil or mean no harm, but trapped all the same and it seeks to take those of us who are willing to step through the light to defeat the darkness that bubbles and boils right below our feet."

Abuela crossed herself and stepped closer to the door. "We are wasting daylight hours talking about this. It's time for some action. What do you have for us today, ladies?"

The morning sun blazed above them. What appeared to be a sleepy little side street in downtown Asheville, with tourists happy to be on their way to the market shops, they would never know what was in the trunk of the Lamborghini of what appeared to be the two oldest women alive in America.

Betty Lou said, "Open up," and the trunk began to rise.

Tyler said, "Oh, that's cool. I want one of those."

"Commission my husband. He has the patent."

Dorothy lifted a blanket, just enough to see the tuft of blond hair peeking out, hair connected to a forehead with the markings 666 etched across it with what appeared to be a crude knife. "We just caught one this morning. Must have been in the cards, fate if you will," Dorothy said.

Abuela said, "All in God's timing. Nothing is left up to coincidence."

"Take us to the site," Father Jacoby said. "There are bound to be more."

Victoria stepped away and looked in every direction but the trunk. "What was that?"

"That, my too young to drive but old enough to cast into the depths of the fiery pit, is a demon possession of a host that is no more."

"We don't do well to them trying to ruin Asheville. They should have known better to try to set up camp here. As you can see, it's tourist season, already."

"But why are they here?" asked Tyler.

"Because you are, my dear. They've hunted you down and tracked you here. And before long, well, you know what that means, Father Jacoby."

Abuela put her arm around Jacoby to steady herself. "They will find us all. This is more serious than I thought, Jacoby."

He whispered, "No fear, My Lita, My Love. There is power in the name of Jesus. We shall overcome."

Tyler said, "For I am the Lord your God who takes hold of your right hand and says to you, do not fear; I will help you."

Dorothy Lamar said, "The power is strong with this one. Did you hear that verse come out of him with such passion, with such a force that takes your breath? Like the wind of a rotating fan you are standing too close against. Ah, this one is ready. He is strong, indeed."

Victoria squeezed Tyler's hand, who then laced their fingers together tightly. She could feel that power through him. His faith had always been a tangible presence between them. It was in his speech, the way he looked at any situation, or how he answered her even in the simplest of conversations that always comforted her. He was her strength and her shield, the one she could depend on in the most difficult of times. The one who made her laugh, even in the face of her most awkward or hurtful moments.

Victoria said, "I'm glad you are my two-by-two."

"Me too," he leaned over to kiss her forehead. "Now, if we're about to go somewhere can I ask a favor?"

Father Jacoby laughed. "I already know what it is."

"Can I ride in the Lambo? It's a bucket list, kinda thing. I've been marking them off lately, and I figure this might be my only chance at this one in life."

"Sure thing, sweet cakes. Hop in."

He went around to open the passenger side door, but Betty Lou stopped him. "I didn't mean you could ride along shotgun. Get in that driver's seat, baby doll. Who am I to stand in the way of a young boy with wild long hair and his dreams?"

"For real?"

Betty Lou said, "For real."

He laughed like a child dropped in the middle of the chocolate factory, "And this is the day that the Lord has made ..."

Abuela finished his sentence this time. "Let us rejoice and be glad in it."

"Rejoice all you want right now, young man. In a few minutes time, you'll come face to face with an evil that either shatters all your senses or builds up your power to face the future."

The smile never left Tyler's face, and as he adjusted the mirrors, fully aware that there was some demon in the trunk but not caring in the least he said, "Until that time, let me enjoy the little things."

Dorothy Lamar took the bag from the back seat and took Father Jacoby's arm, even though he didn't offer it. "I'll ride with the three of you if that is okay. Being cramped up in that back seat will throw out my back. Besides, I have something I'd like to show you, Father Jacoby."

Abuela murmured, "I bet you do."

Betty Lou said, "Follow behind us. It's not too far from here. I'll make sure this boy doesn't lose you around the turns. No pedal to the metal, son. Drive, but a snail's pace is more of the speed this baby needs to go."

"In a Lambo? On mountainous roads with drop-offs that lead into a rocky cavern of explosions if I overcorrect or go too fast around the bend – no problem. I'll slowly, slowly, very slowly creep a garden trail of a snail around the turns."

Victoria said, "Stick to your promises, Tyler."

"You know me, a man of my word." He cranked up the car, and as the engine revved, he let out a Lumbee call, "Kee-kee!"

She snapped a picture of him, the smile on his face one she would remember forever that held all the innocence and love and all things good before he was introduced to pure evil.

Before they would both suffer their first scar.

Praise Before Battle

The Asaph National Forest stretched out before them like the promised land, and it was clear God created the Heavens and the Earth when entering the park. Too much was occurring too fast, and Victoria just wanted it all to slow down. The thought of her life becoming a battle over good and evil, an exorcist, it still had not become part of her identity. She never thought she'd be traveling down winding roads of the paranormal to face God knows what.

Her future remained uncertain, but her resolve must be stronger than her fear. She could see Tyler up ahead, turning every so often to smile at something that Betty Lou said. If he were a part of her future, and if that meant Abri and her family could get their life back, she could face it.

She would be his two-by-two, and that would be no sacrifice at all.

Father Jacoby's excited voice rose above her thoughts, bringing her back to reality. "There is no way that Solomon invented this! Does it work, as you say?"

"Fully tested. Just yesterday. How do you think we found that thing in the back of the trunk?"

"But to track a demon, to pick up a trail of an evil spirit? Oh my God, this is a game changer!"

"He calls it the Uncle Sam, saying it is his patriotic duty to protect America from the wolves knocking on the door. He even made a promotional flyer after that classic propaganda poster and will offer it to the Instrumental Transcommunication community."

Abuela asked, "Is that why they've come here, to Asheville?"

"It tracks, but it doesn't read minds or motives. It will pick up their mumbling speech and catch them unaware."

Victoria said, "When you say they, how many are you talking about?"

Father Jacoby said, "Let's put this baby to the test, shall we." He held it the handheld device up like a new prize. "It's similar in design to my infrared tracker, but the potential in this is great for the field of research. We can gather statistics and have the evidence we need."

"Think about it," Abuela interrupted, "If there is a device that can track the evil within, doesn't that mean if it fell into their hands, they could take that same technology and find those of the light, the remaining of us, and try to end us all."

"Try is the operative word here," answered Dorothy Lamar. "We aren't that taken by the dark."

Victoria said, "Has anyone you know ever fallen away?"

"There are many called, but the laborers are few," Abuela said. "Many have fallen away, not willing to give it all up for the quest for freedom of those in bondage."

Victoria said, "Seems like a rewarding career if you think about it. Helping others who don't have the knowledge, calling, or the power to help themselves."

"It is. If your Abuelo were still alive, he would be the first to line up to tell you he gave all he had to saving lost souls, and would not regret a second of the life we led together."

"You had each other." Victoria thought of Tyler.

Father Jacoby said, "Don't forget about me. I came in handy a time or two."

Victoria asked him, "Where is your two-by-two?"

Father Jacoby didn't answer. Instead, he held up the screen. "If this is accurate, there are four demons just up ahead. Victoria, pray."

"Why now?"

Abuela answered, "Praying when you know you are about to face the biggest test of your life always helps to clear the way."

She turned up the Christian radio station and the song, Praise Before the Battle, roared out of Abuela's Jeep speakers.

Victoria might not have known the words, but she let every lyric sink in. She thought this was the most important test of her life, heavier than final exams or the college entrance tests. The worries of the typical teenager left her. She was to be an exorcist and demons would flee.

As Abuela pulled the Jeep to a stop, she held onto the handle, saying one last prayer before stepping out of the vehicle.

Whatever happens here, God, let it be for you. Amen.

Victoria didn't know if that was what she needed to pray since it was a new concept for her. Would she ever understand it? Was there a ritual to conduct? A splash of holy water for good measure?

She didn't have time to think about what she could have done.

The creature stood still by the line of pines, the dense forest outstretched behind it for over five hundred acres, and she knew how close she was from losing sight of the fiend in the thick green blanket. If this was a place to get lost in, she had found it. Adrenaline flowed from her spirit. It had at first glance the appearance of a human, but everything rose within Victoria to let her know it was not. Far from it.

Her mind flashed to a memory of her and her sister as they played on the sand last summer at Oak Island. Making sand angels, building a princess tower where she could still dream of such things. No more. Not today.

"You messed with the wrong girl," whispered Victoria.

She knew the demon heard her. It raised its head in recognition, nostrils flaring as if to smell her.

"That's right. It's me. Come at me."

Tyler's laughter stopped when he caught her gaze toward the towering, tree line and he saw the demon for himself.

He said aloud, "Our Father, which art in Heaven, hallowed be thy name…"

Standing side by side was Father Jacoby with his bag of tricks, Abuela adjusting her prayer shawl, and the two sisters grasping their canes. In the middle of them were Victoria and Tyler, one held Abuelo's crucifix, the other led the prayer.

They advanced and in unison said, "Lead us not into temptation, but deliver us from evil. For thine is the kingdom and the power, and the glory, forever, amen."

Victoria repeated, "Amen."

The demonic creature stepped backward, disappearing into the woods.

"So, they want to challenge us, do they?" retorted Father Jacoby. "Well, they don't know about this." He held up Uncle Sam and let the coordinates register.

Tyler said, "Let the race begin. Let us run that we may obtain it."

They stepped forward into the unknown, with a guarantee they were not alone. The Spirit of the Lord was with them all, and that would be enough.

****

Dr. Silas Amon could not believe the report. This could not be. Bathin, the father of all lies, was his trusted companion, and it would have been easy to imagine the setback as a trick, but the look on Bathin's face told otherwise. Silas paced the office floor, murderous rage took over his senses, and he knew he could lose himself.

Bathin warned, "You'll burn a hole in the floor with all that pacing."

Silas Amon seethed, "I'll burn a hole in their flesh, their brains. I will eat away at them and tear them apart limb by limb."

The news had traveled fast in the network. Bathin reported, "There is a report that one of ours has been taken, but I fear the others will be captured soon. We need to send out another hunting party to cut their hearts out. At least there is a silver lining to this, Amon."

Silas screamed, and his voice took on the language that only those from hell could decipher. "Give it to me, then! Speak it now before I punish you because of this oversight."

"It is a sign we are close, Lord. It means we are near his hideout. Manuel Ortega could not expect to evade us much longer, and he is the only one left with enough power to come between the girl uniting with the One."

"Power!" He raged and slapped Bathin in the face. "He has no power. He did not cast me to hell when he had his chance. He did not discover my name, and he never will. And it is no longer necessary to refer to her as a girl. It is he. No one will stop the possession. Not even Manuel Ortega."

Amon tore at his suit, rent his clothes in two. Across his rippled red chest were the burn marks of the Marked Ones, the pentagram glowed brighter with his full rage.

Bathin said, "We need to get the plans in order. I think going under the grid might be advisable due to the recent events. We've come too far to jeopardize the change. All of the work you have done will not be in vain."

Realizing he lost control, Amon pulled a new shirt from the closet, sat down at his desk, and felt his composure return. "It's always necessary to have a backup plan, but then again, I've never run away from a good fight."

"It's nothing personal, just protecting the asset."

"True." As he buttoned up his shirt, he felt his face smooth back to its human form. "And that is why I have you here, it seems. To protect me from running with my instinctive nature to those mountains to find that Manuel Ortega, that hoax, and slit his throat with my very fingernails."

"Exactly. I knew I would be good at something. Let's get the preparations in order. I've already secured a new location that I can provide a free flight over to visit at your command. I would like your opinion about a few final touches."

Silas Amon pulled the folder from his desk drawer and ran his hands across the Cambion logo. "Bring the little children unto me," he whispered, "Then, we shall make them burn."

Never Too Late

An intense odor mixed with pine needles and honeysuckle filled the air. If Victoria didn't know better, it would have been a dead carcass of an animal left to the cycle of nature. It smelled of the same rotted meat that no air freshener could mask, the putrid one that circulated through her house and air conditioning duct. The kind she recognized now as demonic. They needed no tracker to know the devil were near. The tell-tale signs were present around them.

It had marked the trees with strange symbols, circles, and lines. Father Jacoby placed his palm across the carvings. "Let's take pictures of the site to mark the patterns for later analysis."

Tyler became the official photographer of the group.

Victoria crunched over stripped animal bones, then jumped back. Dorothy pushed at a bone with her cane. "Sacrifice. Look at that. They ate the raw meat clean off."

Father Jacoby said, "These are the ancient ones that go bump in the night. Brave must be this lot to see the light of day."

"Or stupid," said Abuela, who had already hummed a song, no words needed to know that it must have been an old gospel hymn because Tyler hummed along.

Father Jacoby motioned, then whispered, "To the left. Careful now."

Victoria visualized herself on a military extraction team, sneaking in on terrorist, about to take over a camp. These creatures evoked some kind of terror.

Father Jacoby surprised her. "This is where we stop, and you continue."

Tyler asked, "What do you mean stop? You mean, you aren't going with her?"

"No. You are," answered Betty Lou. "It's your turn to battle the beasts and keep them at bay."

Father Jacoby handed him a bottle of holy water, slipped a prayer book in his back pocket, and patted him on the back. "You've got this son. I believe in you."

Tyler felt weak. "Thanks."

Abuela cradled Victoria's face in her hands. "There is no fear. You cast it aside. You are an Ortega. Manuel's blood flows through your veins, and I know that he is here with you in spirit. More than Manuel, you have Jesus. That is all you need. You are ready, my Neita. Believe, and the faith will set you free."

Tyler grabbed Victoria's hand. "We do this together, you and I."

For the first time since Christmas, when they started what first seemed to be a silly, endearing joke to them became real.

"I need you every hour," she whispered as she stepped in closer to him.

"Every hour of every day."

Victoria heard her grandmother call out, "You will be victorious, for the Lord your God is the one who goes with you to fight for you against your enemies to give you victory."

The rest repeated, "Amen."

When they lost sight of their backup, Tyler whispered, "Nothing like a little hunting to get the blood pumping. I wish I had my running dogs, I bet they could sense out them demons."

They left the tracker, and all the technology behind. If they wanted them in a training session, why couldn't they strap them with VR headgear and let them play a zombie game? That would have felt real enough. This was beyond what Victoria even knew how to describe.

Victoria said, "Far from the exciting plans we had this summer, huh?"

"Yeah, tell me about it. I guess God had other plans for us."

They saw their enemy. Tyler's body tensed beside her but then relaxed when they saw it was only a child. Victoria saw the look of confusion cross the poor, little boy's face. He had bites across his check, his palms were dirty, something tore his pants, and he had no shoes.

Victoria cried out, "Oh, sweetie. Are you lost? Where are your parents?"

The little boy whimpered soft cat-like mewing. He pointed off toward what Victoria picked up as the sound of rushing water. His family must have camped by the river.

"Can we help him, Tyler? I'm sure his family isn't far."

"Are you sure? What if it is a trap?"

"Seriously, Tyler. He is a child."

"So is your sister."

She stepped forward and reached out her hands. She watched as the boy stepped back, then peeked from around a tree at her, still curious if she would harm or help him. "I promise I won't hurt you."

The boy stepped from behind the oak, climbed over the upraised roots and walked down them like a tightrope artist. He grabbed her arm and walked with Victoria towards the river.

Tyler's Spirit moved within him, and he warned Victoria. "I have a strong suspicion he's not lost."

She had the sneaking suspicion he was right. "Me, too."

As they walked ahead, Tyler took the bottle of holy water he slipped in the cargo pocket of his khaki shorts, which he noted came in handy for demon hunting. He popped the cap, and with a flick of his wrist, he splashed it on the boy's back. The water hit his jet-black hair, splattered on the back of his neck, and water lines dripped down his back and underneath his t-shirt.

It was a natural reaction. The muscles tensed and the shoulder blades extended from the unexpected hit. As sudden as the change of the North Carolina weather, the boy dropped to his knees. His shoulders heaved, and the pattern of his breath picked up a pace that could not be normal. It should have caused hyperventilation. Instead, the rhythmic building kept coming in a pant, pant, pant until the demon showed itself, turning to his assailant first, the blackened eyes setting their sights on Tyler if it could even see.

"You stay behind me, boy. Strike me again, and you will see the wrath placed upon your head." The voice was hypnotic, dark and unsettling to come from such a child that size.

"Victoria, pray! Do something!" Tyler said, his voice rising in strength, "For the Lord your God is the one who goes with you to fight for you against your enemies to give you victory."

The burn marks formed where the holy water touched bare skin, boiling a putrid hissing sound of heated flesh. The shock of it overwhelmed her, so surreal that Victoria's heart beat like rumbling thunder in her chest and disorientation hit her, knocked her senses like a silver bullet pinball machine in her brain.

Victoria tried her best to form words, anything she could speak that would make sense, patterned the notes in her Abuelo's journal and found the syllables. In seconds of silence that felt like an eternity, she spoke, "Demon, what is your name? Why are you here?"

"My name is not for you to know. He is stronger than you, you know. Ye of little faith."

"I have the faith the size of a mustard seed, and the Bible says that is all I'll ever need. He will provide the rest of the portion."

The demon said in his sing-song voice, "Oh, the Bible tells me so. How Sunday school of you. Oh, you never went to Sunday school, right? You are weak, but he is strong. You will die. I will ripe your heart out and eat it."

Tyler saw as the demon cowered at her feet when she raised the crucifix and placed it on his forehead. She grasped the back of his head in her hand and held him and the cross together like a vice grip. She prayed, in a voice of calm resolve, as if she had known the words needed for a time such as this.

"Father, heal this child. Remove this demon from this boy, this innocent child of God. He is yours, Lord. Release the hold on his spirit, you demon. I don't need to know your name. I know the name of God, the Father, who created Heaven and Earth."

She pressed harder, and he withed in pain, his voice softened to that of the child's. "But it burns. It hurts me. Momma? Daddy? Where are you? What's wrong? Stop! You're hurting me. Oh, it hurts so bad."

Her voice rose in command with the Spirit, which no demon could deny, "Now, I cast you back to hell, in the name of Jesus Christ and all that is holy, leave this boy. Now!"

They watched as the demon released itself, a dark stream flowed from the boy's mouth and nostrils. He choked and arched his tiny frame, his back contorted and twisted from the pain of the pulling away of the evil curse upon his body. He fell back against the earth, leaves scattered, the thud louder than what they would have expected from such a small child.

Victoria looked to Tyler for some confirmation.

He was unsure of it himself. "Was that it? Did you do it? Is it over?"

"I think so," she said as she knelt over the child. "Oh my God, what if I killed him?"

When he opened his eyes, they were soft and blue. He squinted from the brightness of the sun as it streamed between the canopy of trees. His angelic features returned, the burn marks circling to a slight bubble, like the way carbonated drinks fizz out after the pop of the top. He whimpered in a voice that broke her heart, "Where's Mommy?"

Tyler comforted him. "Shh…it's okay. We will find them. We've got you, little man."

Tyler lifted the boy in his arms and turned back. The boy smoothed down Tyler's hair, fascinated that it was so long and silky. Victoria watched the two for a moment, shock still coursed through her system. She tried to focus on the tenderness he displayed and realized how close he had come to losing himself, and it made her want to cry.

Victoria stopped him as he stepped toward the rushing sounds of the river, more noticeable now as her head cleared. "We can't go that way with him. He can't see his family like that if the same thing has befallen them. Let's take him to Father Jacoby and Abuela. They will know what to do."

The need to go towards the river seized her. She knew they were there, the rest. Waiting. Planning.

"Victoria, let's hurry."

"I'm coming." She glanced behind her shoulder every other step, wondering if they were coming for her, but nothing was there.

Thank you, God, for saving that boy.

Tyler called back, "His name is James. He said his family was on a camping trip, and he thinks he just got lost. That's all he remembers."

"I pray it stays that way, losing all memory of that is the best thing for them." She remembered the journal of her grandfather and the anecdotal records and realized this boy would be the first exorcism she conducted. She would write about him soon enough.

"Ask him how old he is."

Tyler said, "He is only six years old."

"The youngest," she said. "He has been the youngest."

Her soul burst with such emotion. A young child attacked by evil, fraught with the same disastrous end as Abri if they hadn't been present.

How dare the devil fool himself that he could win. She knew the ending of the Bible. Tyler had the ultimate spoiler alert and told her that Satan loses. How dare Lucifer think for one minute she would allow it to take another soul on her watch?

"Never again," she prayed, "Lord, let it be where in your name all demons flee and mercy rains."

"That sounds like a new song lyric. Maybe we have a business in the Christian music industry, we can leave the rock behind."

"We could be a mix of the two," she said. This conversation put her at ease. It brought her comfort in the middle of what would appear to be a desperate situation.

"That's a good idea, maybe a Southern Christian Rock mix. You got that country slang, too. Let's throw that in."

The conversation turned to an abrupt halt when they heard a commotion in the trees ahead. "I thought we were walking James away from danger, not carrying him straight into the pit."

Dorothy Lamar called out, "It's just us. What you got there? A little sprout. Just a sweet pea."

Tyler set the shaken boy on his feet, "He lost his way, can you keep him safe until we find his family?"

Victoria mouthed behind his back, "He had a demon. I exorcized my first demon."

Abuela clapped. "Well done. Three to go, dear. Radar shows river action. We send you off again. This little one will be safe with us."

Tyler ruffled the hair of the little boy and said, "Don't you worry about a thing, little man. I'll be back for you in no time." He went over to Father Jacoby's bag and pulled out a cross necklace. "In the meantime, wear this. The Lord will protect you."

James said, "Okay." He held up the cross, trying to look at it but his eyes crossed. "Who is that man hanging there?"

Abuela took the child by the hand. "That my dear child is Jesus. You ever heard about Jesus."

As they walked back to the forest, they could hear the soft lull of James' voice, so different from the demon one that had lived within minutes before. "Who was he?"

"So many people need to know Him, don't they," whispered Victoria.

She thought of the weight she carried before knowing Jesus. She loved Tyler, her family, and her selfish needs. Now she loved the stranger in the coffee shop she watched comfort a friend who was going through a rough time. She loved the little boy, James. She loved the sisters and Father Jacoby, yet Victoria just met them. That was the greatest change in her above anything she could recognize, the love was there without having to force it. It just was. And it was not selective. It was genuine love for all.

Victoria knew that if she lived through this day, it would be the one to tell Tyler all of how she felt, her love for him growing beyond explanation. Would he be able to love her in return? She never would have guessed as they stepped into the clearing that Tyler thought the same thing.

Victoria gripped his hand. She turned to him and gazed in his dark brown eyes. His presence brought her strength. It gave her hope. Somehow, she knew at that moment they would make it.

She said, "I need you every hour."

"Every hour, of every day."

"What verse do you have for me right now. I need a good one."

He thought for a second. "They are all good."

They stepped towards the calming crackle of the campfire wood, prickling, and sizzling. "Well, pick one."

"He began to send them forth two by two and gave them power and authority over unclean spirits."

She saw the father first by the bank of the river. He sat rocking back and forth, his leg dangled as if cracked through at the femur. His strength alone must have allowed him some time with the demon before total control. He did not cower at her feet, and the holy water only agitated him. The reaction wasn't as harsh, but still present, and she knew something afflicted him.

"I cast you out, unclean spirit. In the name of Jesus, leave this man."

Tyler cataloged off verses as he held up the cross against the woman fiend twisting towards him. The demon grabbed Tyler by the throat and lifted him off his feet, his boots dangled and popped against each other.

"Do not touch him, demon. Release him." Victoria took the bottle of holy water from his side pocket and flung it at the creature, weakening her just enough to release the hold on Tyler.

Tyler rubbed his throat and messaged his voice back into full power. "Blessed be the name of the Lord from this time forth and always. From the rising of the sun unto the going down of the same, the Lord's name is to be glorified in every place on Earth and Heaven. The Lord is high above all nations, and his glory above all things."

"You will release your hold upon this father and mother."

She turned to Tyler, "Look at him. He's mangled. What are we going to do?"

The father turned to them, his back contorted, spine popped, sounds ripped. "You will do nothing but fall to the One, bow to the One that has come to save."

"Man, hear me. Your son, James, he needs you."

He slithered off the rock like a snake, coiled and convulsed along the grass and pebbled rocks on the ground. His leg stuck out at a grotesque angle, dragging behind him as he moved his arms to pull his body along to come closer to them.

She could see the flit of the eyes, from full black to edges of the turquoise iris. "Fight it," she continued, "Fight in the name of the Father, and the Son and the Holy Spirit, amen and amen. Demon, I command you, in the name of Jesus Christ, leave this man."

She placed both of her hands on his face, and prayed, "I ask you, God. Save this man. Release the hold of the demon. I cast you out, unclean spirit, in the name of Jesus."

Tyler pulled her away as the vapor burst forth. It spread across her face, but could not enter. The burnt smell made her gag and heave against the dirt. Poisonous fumes returned back to the pits of hell where they were born.

"Victoria, stand up!"

As soon as she got to her feet, two more demons charged at them. The slow walking zombie VR simulation could have never prepared her for the quick and erratic movements of the devils, she understood now why that would be a waste of time. They galloped, arms outstretched, and pushed their way across the campsite, hell-bent demonic horses at her. Both female. Then, she realized the demons were not a he or a she. They knew nothing of such classifications, just that they had a host to live in long enough to do what they set out to accomplish.

One of them could have once been James' mother. She knew she may still be in there fighting, just like the father, coming to his senses on the ground.

Victoria held up the crucifix in front of her as a shield and prayed, "Lord, keep these women still. Hold them in your loving hand. Protect them and remove these demons from them. In Jesus' name and in the power of his blood, release them."

The smaller of the two dropped to her knees, the sound of bone-cracking split the air as she fell against a rock. The bone pierced the skin, but it materialized no pain, no wails of agony. Her only the covering of ears at the mention of the power of the blood of Christ.

The other slowed but did not stop, rose to full height, its head moving from side to side.

It spoke in a hiss, gurgling tones drowning in water. "Where is Manuel? Who is this pathetic thing?"

Victoria almost spoke but knew that it would be a mistake. She wouldn't be manipulated by a demon twice in one day. "Get out of this daughter of Christ, I cast you out."

"She is no daughter of Jesus of Nazareth. She welcomed me in, she invited me in. Most do."

"Then, it's my turn to uninvite you. Leave, you unclean spirit, I command you in the name of Christ."

Just then, she saw that the others had arrived, minus Betty Lou and the boy. Abuela knelt down beside the father and helped him to his feet as best as she could with Jacoby's help.

"Follow me," Abuela said. "I'll take you to your son. Don't look. Eyes to the ground. Come on."

Dorothy and Tyler distracted the demon long enough for Victoria to grab it by the wrists to lock them together with the crucifix in between.

"Not the marks of Christ. Do not burn me there. Anywhere but there. They will not heal, and I will be made a mockery."

Victoria commanded. "In the name of Jesus Christ, the son of the Most High God, and with the power of the Holy Spirit given to me by Christ, I demand you leave this woman now. Demon, leave."

Tyler caught the woman as all life within her gave way. She grew limp and lay helpless in his arms. Her body jerked like a fish out of the water as the black smoke rose from her nostrils and her upturned mouth, distorted with the shape of the ungodly.

Dorothy Lamar knelt beside her cooing, "Come back, sister. Find your way back."

Tyler lowered her to the ground and watched as Father Jacoby started mouth to mouth resuscitation. He called for Tyler to give him the defibrillator and switch it on if need be. Now it made sense why he carried medical supplies and all those bags for any situation he would be prepared.

Victoria ran to see the bone protrude from the ankle of the beast still lying by the rock and knew it would take a lot of healing before this woman had full function again. Dorothy Lamar grabbed the hair of the demon and pulled, wrapping her cane into the length of it.

Victoria pressed the crucifix against its upraised forehead and spoke, "Leave this woman, now, you viper. You cursed thing."

"Never."

"That's a long time for me to torture you, unclean spirit because I will pray at you without ceasing. I will call upon the name of the Lord, forever. His name is higher, he is mighty. God hear me, and grant the power in me by the grace of the Holy Spirit to remove this demon from this woman. In the name of Christ, begone."

She heard the man cry out from the tree line to the clearing, dragging his leg behind him. "Tonya! What's going on, baby? What are you doing?"

It was his wife. James' mother.

Her voice rose over the panicked pleas of the confused father. "James needs you. He is crying for his mother. Come back for James. Please come back for James."

"James is dead. They are all dead. Everyone is dead. Soon you will be dead, too. Do you want me to tell you how you die? I know. I will tell you."

She turned to Tyler, and her heart thundered in her chest, pushing at her rib cage.

Tyler said, "It is a liar, a master of deception." He pointed to the woman who had just regained consciousness. Her body was limp and crumpled.

Tyler knelt down to face the demon. "Woman, you are in there. You must submit yourself to God. Resist the devil, and he will flee from you."

Victoria pressed again. "I cast you out, you unclean spirit. I cast you back to hell. In the name of Christ, you can no longer stay and hold this woman captive any longer. Amen."

A wave of smoke billowed forth, but by this time they knew the drill. Dorothy shook the cane loose from the nape of her neck. They all stepped back as she crumbled to the ground. The man made his way to her, both with a leg dragging and her ankle bone protruding, what a pair. He lowered himself on the ground by her head up to place it on his lap.

"Tonya, we have to find James. Sweetheart, come back to us."

She croaked, her voice still hoarse from the strain, "What happened? Oh my God, my ankle. It hurts so bad!"

Father Jacoby said, "Call the ambulance Dorothy Lamar. Do you still know if Scottie is on the ASPs Squad? Let him in on the latest development so we can clean this up."

Father Jacoby helped up the father again, "This time. Stay up. My back can't take all this up and down."

Tyler picked up the woman, the other still dazed but able to walk beside Dorothy. They followed Abuela back through the forest, to the paved road that led Victoria to her first trip to hell on Earth. She knew she could never go camping after that encounter. All needed medical treatment and fast. The ambulances were on the way to meet them by the trail marker. In twenty minutes time, that would be long enough to figure out how to craft a story about the injuries. Demons not included.

"How could we explain this? What do we say?" asked Tyler.

The man replied, "I don't even know what happened. What happened to my leg? To her ankle? And James? He has these marks on his neck. What's going on?"

Abuela said, "Some things are better left unexplained, and we hope you'll leave it at that, walk away from today and know the truth of how Christ came to deliver the lost. We heard these loud sounds. A crash by the river. There must have been a fall. That is no lie. Go, and take care of your family. We send you in peace, but you must promise me you will consider your family's salvation"

The man said, "What was wrong with Tonya? Was she ill?"

Father Jacoby said, "It was her soul in jeopardy, nothing physical."

James gave Victoria a hug and leaned over from her arms to grab Tyler's hair and tousled it in return. "Can I keep this?" The child held up the oversized cross around his neck.

Father Jacoby nodded in approval. "Of course, you can, little man."

James held up the cross and said, "Hey, dad! This is Jesus."

The man's eyes grew misty as if he understood what had happened back at the campsite. "Yes son, it is."

He turned his head towards his wife, and he watched her as the tears streamed down her face. She explained the fall the best she could to the EMT but having no recollection of how it happened created quite a mystery.

James jumped from Victoria into his father's arms.

"I guess it's never too late to learn the truth now is it, buddy."

Father Jacoby said, "No sir, it is never too late."

He embraced his child and turned to them. "How can I ever thank you enough?"

Abuela said, "You already did. And the good news today is that your son is a believer."

He said, "When something like that back there, whatever that was back there happens, you have no other choice but to believe. If there is a hell, that means there is a heaven, too. Right?"

"Right," answered Victoria. "I'm new at all of this, too, but I want to tell you it's the best feeling in the world knowing I am walking with God. I might not know it all today, but believing is a start. The rest will come with time."

"It is best for you to take your family to church, dedicate your life to serving God, and get baptized."

Those were Father Jacoby's last words to the father as they lifted him up on the stretcher, a splint board positioned on his leg. The ambulances took the family away. The campsite would remain untouched, and fire embers would die out. The orange and gray tents would fall over in time. There was nothing worth returning for, they left with each other. That was enough.

James waved from the window of the ambulance.

Victoria asked, "Is that what Abuelo did it for? For people like them?"

Abuela put her arm around Victoria. "Yes, my Nieta. He said he never regretted a single day, a single battle, even the last one that took his life."

She turned the crucifix over and read, "September 15, 2007, the day that my grandfather died?"

Abuela said, "Yes. That is correct."

Tyler asked, "Is that why this one never made it to the wall? The job was not finished?

Father Jacoby said, "Such a smart young man, full of the Lord, verses, and a heck of an intuition."

Victoria clasped the metal in her hands. "I will be the one to finish it. For souls like those, for God. For Abuelo."

Dorothy said, "I hate to break up the motivational speech, but has anyone forgotten about the demon in the trunk?"

"Oh, that," Betty Lou said, "That is a gift for my husband."

Abuela said, "Couldn't you be normal, like buy him a set of cufflinks?"

Betty Lou laughed. "That would be too boring. Besides, what do you give a man who already has everything he ever wanted?"

Tyler leaned in close to Victoria's ear. She shivered by his closeness. "Don't think that's the way you can impress me, bagging me a demon."

She smiled. "No worries. I think I got you figured out by now. You are a simple man. A hunting licenses. A new shotgun. A pair of snake boots, just the way I like it."

Victoria knew she couldn't waste another day. She vowed to God to live the day she had at hand. A new Victoria, one changed and refined, sharpened by the fire.

As they made their way out of the Asaph National Forest, Victoria said to no one in particular. "I am an exorcist."

Picking Up Pieces

So much was in disarray. Where to start? No matter where the Hartwell's turned, the emptiness of the house shook the core of them both. The laundry basket held piles of clothes to be folded and the soiled bed sheets in the corner stacked as high as the windowsill held their odor as the Garden spiders crawled between the folds. The exterminator had come and gone but hadn't rid the house of the spiders who seemed to desire to live here more than any member of his family ever would again.

Adoria said, "Six months is a long time to be away from her. She will miss the first half of eighth grade."

Gideon frowned. "If we would have left her here, she would've been in no condition to go to school, period. We have to trust that this is the right thing we're doing. In the meantime, we need to get the house in order. Get ready for the transition home."

When she looked around the living room, he wondered what she saw. Did she see the way their life once made sense and blocked out the nasty condition of things now? What do you think of when I leave you here all alone, and what do you do to pass all this time away?

Gideon glanced down at the pile of mental disorder manuals she had purchased since the diagnosis. He picked up Dealing with DID: The Teenage Perspective and flipped through the pages. He turned to the chapter titled Causes and flipped through the headings: Trauma, Assault, Abuse, Neglect. It went on and on.

None of it was adding up. His family was fine six months ago. Well, fine was such a subjective word. They were okay. They functioned at what he considered the typical family. He worked. He came home. He drove the kids to soccer practice and volleyball camp when Adoria checked out, too drained to drive. They had crock pot meals, and he grilled out every Saturday. He made enough so that Adoria didn't have to work. They could still live in the subdivision and drive the car she wanted, buy the clothes the girls wanted. What else to family was there?

Adoria overplayed any situation. She would go to the extreme, now she had a label, a name she could call that thing that was not his daughter once living upstairs. When he saw the stacks of books, he thought he just might pick up all of the contents of the coffee table and throw them all in the Wednesday trash pickup. His daughter wasn't ill. His daughter did not have alternate personalities. Gideon refused to accept it.

Adoria called his stage denial. He chalked that up to something she'd read.

He called it an outrage they would tell him the news of this importance over a telephone call, not even a conference call, where he could at least see some compassion. Just a dry phonecall that let them know that Abrianna would be with them receiving intensive therapy and undergoing medication trials for the next six months for severe DID. Nothing followed, "Do you have any questions or concerns?" or "Sorry to have to break this to you over the phone?" or even a "Have a nice day."

That left Gideon to pick up the pieces of his wife, who for all he knew was back at her round of depression. She had failed as a mother and refused to see the signs. The help could've come sooner, and maybe it wouldn't have escalated to where they lost control of their own home, not to mention fearing for their safety. The whole should've, would've, could've game was old hat at the Hartwell home. Never solved a single problem, and he was sure it never would.

She sighed, her burdens too much to carry. "I think I need to call somebody."

"Your mother? Your daughter? Have you checked on Victoria?"

"No, my counselor. Will you go with me this time?"

This time. How many times was she going to do this, and now she would drag him along to hear all about parenting psychosis Forget that.

"You call all you want. Go and do your thing. You know that's not my style. Lying out on some smelly, germed-up couch and talking about the secrets of our family will not get me where I need to be going."

Adoria's anger flashed, her resentment for him building once more. "And where is that, exactly?"

"To work."

He picked up his briefcase and left out of the house, without their kiss goodbye. That routine of leaving the house without a kiss or suffer the consequences was over long before Adrianna fell sick. The house was no longer a home. He felt like he was living a life that was no longer his own, and he'd no longer put up the pretenses. Would that be what he would tell the therapist? Gideon knew that wouldn't go over too well with Adoria.

He didn't blame her. Or could he? Both of them put in too much time on the trivial things that never amounted to much. For all intents and purposes, if he evaluated his own life, he could sum it up by speaking about the void in his life, the day in day out loss. He couldn't remember the last time the house held any smiles or when he laughed. Period.

Gideon contributed his mood to a lack of sleep. Since he dropped off Abrianna, all he could hear when he tried to close his eyes was the whisper of the children following him out the door. "She is here."

What did that mean anyway? This taunting of a patient, like in prison movies? The eyes of Dr. Silas would also haunt him in his dreams, often when awake, right in the middle of a sales pitch for the marketing team. He would do all in his power to push the thoughts out of his mind and wipe the sweat on his brow that would form every time an episode happened.

It was unnerving. Unnatural.

It dawned on him what he'd done and shame brought him to tears. They left her there to die.

Go get her.

Now.

He swore he heard the words from the backseat. He adjusted the mirror, turned his head sharp feeling a pain seared up his right side. No one was there. Oh, my God. He was going crazy. His right ear buzzed with a ringing noise he couldn't shake. Was he now the one to hear the voices? What would Adoria's books say about that?

Without warning, he turned off westbound I-40 that led him into the Research Triangle Park and made a loop back east. He needed another road, I-95. The one that would take him to his daughter and get her out of whatever it was he left her in. Adoria would be of no comfort on the eight hours there. They would fight, he would relent, and they would go back to pretending. No more.

Gideon would take this trip alone.

The harder he pushed on the accelerator, the faster he came to understand that it was his only option. He could find her care close to home. Just not there. Not there with those chants, those children, those eyes.

Anywhere but there.

Stand with Me

The mansion could not be seen from the twisted road or the entryway, but the type of gated fences that people often wondered what lay behind it if they happened to cross one in their lifetime rose before them. Scrolled within the metal bars, the logo of the ASPs was seen, with the emblem of the snake, and a totem. Tyler had opted out of the Lamborghini experience to stay close to Victoria on the ride out of the forest.

The symbol piqued his interest. "See, there is an official logo, and you guys said I was crazy for wanting a decal for the van. We can get our own matching tattoos. It has to be a Native American symbol, though. We are both under the sign of the bear. We could do a paw or claw."

Abuela said, "Solomon St. Pierre is pretentious."

Victoria exhaled when she saw the residence in front of her. It looked more like a French country house, a manor from a faraway place. "And rich."

Father Jacoby added, "And my dear and most loyal friend. Even though he reigns on the tacky side, his heart is as pure as gold, and he would give the shirt off his back to help a poor, lost soul."

Abuela said, "He has this fetish with collecting objects of absurdity, oddities if you ask me. Don't say we didn't warn you, try your best to hold in your shock."

Tyler asked, "So, that's why she kept the demon? For a collection? But isn't there a soul in there? A person needing to be freed from bondage?"

The moans were louder now, the dance of the demon in the trunk pounded against metal and seat.

Victoria said, "Let's pull the devil out of it before we take it inside. We can't just let it suffer."

They got out of the car, and Betty Lou waited patiently by the trunk.

Father Jacoby asked, "Aren't you going to open it?"

She said, "I want to see the look of surprise on his face. He's coming. Just has to come in from his morning run. He is on the trail. Like clockwork, that man's routine is. I could map him out by the minute."

Victoria took in her surroundings. They had a line of red luxury cars parked by an ornate fountain. The flag was raised high, bearing the ASPs logo.

Victoria loved symbolism, a strength her English teacher, Mrs. Aiken, often called out that she could recognize in the short story collections and novels they read. But the snake allusions didn't quite fit the elders she knew, or what they stood for.

She asked, "Why the symbols?"

Abuela answered, "So those like us know they are safe when they enter here. Those of the Way travel far to study with us, to sit with us and learn how to best serve the Lord with the special gifts we have."

Father Jacoby said as the door opened, "This is a stronghold of sorts, and inside lives the most technologically advanced of our kind. He has taken ITC to the next level."

The elderly man that stood in tight, way too short blue and white running shorts, high tube socks with pink colored lines, and a white polo shirt was the most advanced of their kind? He wore a thin headband with matching wristbands, looking like he might have stepped out of an advertisement for a tennis racket from days gone by.

Betty Lou said, "I love a sweaty man, and that's my man."

He raised his hand in greeting, and a smile spread wide when he saw them all there. "Ah, my favorite kind of day. The one that includes my lovely wife, and Jacoby Wethington. Hello, my old friend."

"Who you calling old?" answered Jacoby. "You've got a good twenty years on me and still kicking it in the coolest way. If only I can get around at your age, much less run the mile, I'll be good to go."

Solomon said, "Three miles a day. The day I run a mile, is the day it might be the last of my race."

He kissed his wife and said, "Why are y'all standing out here? Come on inside. I'll have Maggie whip us up something light for lunch, and we can catch up on the times. Adelita, such a grand pleasure. And who might these beauties be, such beauty is in youth, and if you keep it, you never grow old."

Abuela said, "This is Manuel's granddaughter, Victoria Elizabeth Ortega Hartwell, and her two-by-two, Tyler Locklear."

He eyed them both quizzically and turned to Father Jacoby. "They know of this life?" He waved his hand nonchalantly as if it were the norm.

"Nice to see you, too, Sol," said Dorothy Lamar, "We just came back from an exorcism, if that is what you mean. While you've been getting your cardio, we've been doing a spiritual workout against the fiends of hell."

"Speaking of, my dear. I brought you a little something. A memento, so to speak. Open up."

His immense pleasure spread across his face, and he did a little two-step in abundant joy. "Oh, baby. You caught me a live one. Really? It's for me?"

"All for you, dear. All for you."

He turned to Father Jacoby. "That again is proof that she is the love of my life."

He pulled what appeared to be a tiny speaker from the chain around his neck and spoke into it. "Egor, we need some assistance at the front. Bring the SAM Transport."

Tyler asked, "You have someone that works for you named, Egor?"

Abuela smirked. "If you pay someone enough, they will change their name to Barney. I told you, pretentious."

"Maybe a little. Now, come inside and have some tea. Where I am pretentious, I am also generous. What is mine is yours at le chateau de l'ASPS."

Egor, or whoever he was, pulled a dolly welded into a cage. A burly man that reminded Victoria of the Cossack brute from the short story she read in the 9th grade, The Most Dangerous Game. Victoria watched as he lifted the demon as if it were a small wounded animal and locked it up in the portable cage.

Did he whistle as he came toward them? The creaking of the wheels turning round screeched and rattled her senses, like fingernails across the chalkboard. She reached for her Abuela and grabbed her arm. Were they going to explain this? This collection? And why did Betty Lou, who seemed so gentle and reserved, find a thrill in monster hunting when a soul was captured there?

It was too late to turn back. They all entered into the foyer. The beauty of the hewn rocks and natural elements of the stones stopped at the exterior. Inside was a dark and brooding atmosphere, a step back into what could only be explained as medieval. The hat and coat rack were an actual guillotine with a certificate of authenticity framed beside it, dating it to 1792 with the name Dr. Joseph Ignace Guilloti etched in the brass plate.

An Uncle Fester look-alike appeared in the hallway to collect Betty Lou's things and took the bags that Father Jacoby carried. Old black and white movie posters lined the walls, not family portraits or paintings of the house of those who Victoria would have considered normal. What was normal anymore? Who was she to judge?

"Bienvenue to my house of horrors," he announced as they passed by a room devoted to some of the most iconic films of all time. It was as it should be in a place like this. Instead of a game room with lines of trophy hunts he had killed on worldly excursions, he had mannequins dressed, posed in an elaborate wax museum. Watching serial killer marathons were chilling enough, a tradition that she and Tyler had started as soon as their parents allowed them to watch scary movies, but a real-life like replica of the most notorious in history lined in front of her, never mind that. Not in her house.

Next, they all were led into the library. It was as if they had stepped right into the set of the original Pharaoh's Mummy. Egyptian artifacts were encased wall to wall, and Victoria did not question their authenticity. She read that the mummy in the guided glass case was from 1507 B.C. and that he probably should have been in a Cairo museum, instead of the middle of a hideaway villa in Asheville.

These kinds of archeological finds should have been for the world to see, and she felt honored that she had a glimpse of the past she loved to study so up close and personal. The library was massive, the collection weathered with time as the mummies that surrounded her. The ladders extended from the ceiling, with small roller ball wheels attached. Oh, how she dreamed of those when she was a child, to be like Belle and ride the ladders of a grandiose library.

But this library was not filled with books about fairies of the Tinker Bell kind, or the stories where farm boys would become dragon riders. Instead, these were the books where evil lived. A collection of demonology texts, codecs, and dark, religious books filled every space, alphabetized and ordered by topic. Maybe Victoria would cross off the library twirl around the room off her to-do list for the day.

The connecting room behind a moveable library shelf appeared to be a lab, and Father Jacoby appreciated the layout. "Next to the library, research can be partnered with scientific pursuits. I like what you've done to the place. A little on the primitive side if you ask me, you might consider another decorator."

"Oh, the jokes, always full of them aren't you, Jacoby. I knew you would appreciate this room. Why don't you stay with me here while I show you some of my latest inventions? The top gear in the industry is right behind those locked cases. The rest of you go ahead and tour Betty Lou's side of the house. You'll probably find it more of your taste. I need my surroundings to help keep me creative."

Betty Lou kissed him on the cheek. "Yes, dear. I'll have Maggie bring up your lunch. We will return in a little while and give the two of you a chance to catch up." She leaned closer to Solomon, "He needs some prayer time with you, honey. His heart is too heavy to bear."

Victoria was close enough and the only one to hear her whisper, and it made her wonder why a priest close to God would have a burden.

They walked down the long corridor and just as it was about to never end, it turned a sharp ninety-degree angle to the right.

Victoria let out an appreciative sigh that echoed down the hall. "Now, this is more like it."

Betty Lou said, "I always get that reaction. Seems like he would have started with my half of the house first and only saved his fanciful to those of that taste. It is an acquired one, I must say so myself. But it's a modern-day twist on the old 'his and hers' concept."

Victoria said, "I think a set of towels or matching coffee cups with 'his and hers' works for me."

Abuela eyes crinkled in the corners from her smile. "Let the youngsters take their time in the garden. They've hardly had a chance to breathe. You did well today. Now, for the time being, go relax. We have the biggest battle of our lives to face soon enough. In the meantime, try to rest and spend some prayer time together. You will need to reserve your strength for the days to come."

Betty Lou disappeared behind a swinging door. She returned a few minutes later with a basket made for Victoria and Tyler. She pointed. "Go out through the patio doors. You may eat on the deck or in the gardens. Whichever you prefer."

Victoria leaned over to Abuela and asked, "Is it safe?"

"Safe compared to what? Today? I think most places are, dear."

Dorothy already had an old jazz tune trumpeting out of the antique phonograph. She leaned back on the shabby chic couch and propped her feet up. "I'm eating right here. Serve me up, sister. I don't think I will move until I'm forced to do so, or removed by crane, whichever comes first."

Abuela said, "Suit yourself."

Tyler opened the door for Victoria, and she stepped out into the sunlight.

She took in all the beauty. Such vile memories of torment an hour ago needed to be erased from her mind. Victoria wondered if Father Jacoby had a gadget in his bag to take care of unwanted images still pulsed in her brain. The intensity of the gardens stretched before her reminded her that God made things like this. He had no likings for those other creatures in the world, and that is why and only why she could cast them out.

Victoria said, "Does this make you want to cry? A day like today. Knowing it is still going on around us. And now we step out here as if nothing else exists but beauty."

"It makes me want to eat, that's all."

She grinned. "Of course, you do. Too bad there isn't a Cook's around here."

"With this kind of dinero, I bet we could get some flown in." He picked up his cellphone and started to imaginary call, changing his voice to a terrible impersonation of a British accent. "Cheerio, young man. Mi mucho hungry at the Casa de la ASP. Arrive with two of your latest burger and taco boxes, a side of nachos, and as much Caliente sauce as you can stuff in a bag."

"I think you told Cook's goodbye before you even started the conversation. You do know that was what cheerio actually meant, right?"

"Money talks, no one corrects." Tyler reminded her.

There was a stone patio for entertaining a large crowd, and a gazebo a few yards away trellised with wisteria vines. The crisscross patterned lawn went on for at least a mile then the line of the forest stood guard, mountain peaks scaled the distance. There were French garden walkways that lead east or west as you stepped off the redwood deck.

"So, where to start, which way to walk? Pick a spot because I honestly want to explore it all. I feel like I need an umbrella and a pair of lace gloves."

"It does seem as if we are in another world. Far from Raleigh, I sure know that."

Tyler decided to go right and led her to the gated entryway into the butterfly garden trail. Every few steps, they walked under metal trellises laced with white and red, large bloomed flowers that hung overhead. It was a well-kept garden on both sides of the brick and stone walkway, with layers upon layers of colorful flowers and bushes.

Stone statues of angels of all shapes and sizes guarded their walk. Bible verses were etched in stone and mortared into the brick walls. Birdbaths were positioned by the line of bluebird houses. This must be a place to go to escape it all. Victoria decided she could live there. The songwriting she could do in a place like this. If this was Solomon's idea as a gift for his wife, Victoria at least appreciated the train of thought he had in that mind.

She said, "It's like he must be some kind of Dr. Jekyll and Mr. Hyde character. I can't imagine him taking his early morning jog through this then walk back to his lab to test paranormal equipment."

Tyler agreed. "We all have two sides to us but come to think of it, I am probably more like an Indian nickel."

"And what is that?"

"It's a nickel spent the same as any, but just a different mint. One side Indian, one side buffalo, except my other side of the coin would have my spirit. There is no separating me from the Spirit. When I was created new, I was created one with Him."

He placed the basket down on a bench near the Lantanas. She didn't know how to identify all of the garden varieties, but she did recognize these from her mother's garden. Well, the one that used to be kept in the corner by the fence line, before their family was ripped apart by a demon in disguise of a long, haired soft faced beautiful girl.

She tried to push her thoughts back to live in the present. She made a promise to God that she would do just that. Victoria didn't realize just how hard that promise might be to keep.

She focused her attention on Tyler. "You do have a way about you, you know. I didn't notice how strong until all of this."

Tyler unwrapped the sandwiches and passed her aside. "What do you see?" He glanced quickly at her and then turned away.

"You always have talked about the Lord in conversations, like it would pop up at random times and to be honest with you I never really listened. I'm sorry for being so blind and ignoring you."

"I was blind, but now I see. You see now, that's what matters. There is a change in you, I see it now, too."

"Well, the last time you saw me, I wasn't wearing the name tag exorcist. My new summer job might not bring any money to my bank account, but if the Lord is counting works for the saving of souls a worthy vocation, then I guess I'm in the best job around."

He asked, "How did you pray like that?"

"Like what?"

"Back there. It took me years to get comfortable with praying out loud, as sad as it is to say that. Even though I could repeat scriptures from Bible drills at church, you know I was once the state champ, but when it came to praying out loud, I would just freeze."

"I don't know where it came from. Just the words poured out, and I let them. I wasn't even thinking of it or planning out words in my head. Just let whatever was meant to be said to come out."

He said, "That makes me think of Stephen. You haven't read about him yet, he is in the next book, the book of Acts. He was the first martyr, preaching full of faith and the Holy Spirit."

"What happened to Stephen?"

"Maybe we should save that conversation for later," he said.

Victoria said, "Maybe it isn't me talking at all. That's the part where it means comforter, isn't it? It's a comfort that I don't have to think of the right things to say. The Lord will provide all I need in my time of trouble."

"You are amazing, you know that."

Victoria looked at him. She wanted to say so much to him, had so many thoughts about life, faith, love, all running through her mind at once until she felt lightheaded from the intensity of it. How she loved the way his pitch-black hair, with the highlighted strands he let her die fell long past his shoulders, reflected the sunlight in a myriad like a thick cloud.

She wanted to say how she admired his strength, his honesty. How he always made her laugh, and even if no one else in the world found him funny, she did. She loved how he knew her. How she could truly be herself with him, and he accepted everything about her, even this.

Something so hard to even fathom existed, but he was sitting here with her. He had stood with her in the pines, facing the evil for her. When they were smaller, she didn't need a world of friends, a following, or a fan club. All she had ever needed was him, and their bond was eternity shaped, infinite.

She couldn't say any of that. All she could whisper was, "I need you every hour."

"Every hour of every day."

And she meant it now more than ever before. She wondered if he did, too.

Be Still

He didn't drop to his knee. There were no fireworks in the distance, concert music blaring in the background or a rehearsed speech. But it was the perfect moment as any, and he knew today had to be the day to risk it all. There were the chirping sounds of the Cardinals, the music the wind makes in weeping willow trees, chimes clanging in the distance, and God all around.

Tyler put his hand in his pocket and felt the tiny, white antique box he had been carrying for the past year. His sentimental mother lent him the jewelry case. Lord help her. It had held the wedding rings of his grandparents. She removed those for safekeeping and the purity ring nestled in their place on the green velvet.

He would ask her now. Tyler prayed, *God, help me be strong and say the right things so she'll know how much I love her.*

Tyler heard the still small voice of the Spirit. Be still and know that I am God.

"Victoria, I need to ask you something?"

"Shoot."

Before he could get the next words out, two soft-yellow, almost white butterflies danced from the bush to hover around Victoria. Her eyes widened with simple joy, and her body tensed as if she didn't want to stir with the slightest movement to frighten them away. One fluttered to a stop and landed on her hair, near her cheek. She could see the outline of it and took in her breath. The other seemed to want to move between her and Tyler before finally resting on her arm, tickling her with its delicate movements.

Tyler pulled out his phone to snap. "I caught them for you."

"They are another two-by-two. Like us."

"Maybe so."

The minutes passed between them in silence. Mesmerized by the dance of nature and the knowing that love lived true between them.

Tyler grinned and looked up at the sky. "Who needs a firework show, when God's work does so much better at showing off. Perfect timing, by the way."

"For what?"

He pulled out the box and placed it on her thigh. "For this."

"And when did you have time to go get me a gift? In between soul rescue one or two?"

"Just open it."

Victoria clicked open the latch of the delicate box. A sound escaped, but she could not speak. She didn't want to read too much into this. Was it just an early birthday present? Her heart raced and she could feel the heat rising in her cheeks.

"When I bought this, I knew it was perfect, but I didn't know how perfect it was until right now. Shows me again how God had this planned before me."

Her finger traced the two silver connecting hearts, small diamonds encasing the trail. "A two by two?"

"Baby, I can't tell you how much of an honor it brings God chose me to be that for you, to be your companion for whatever this will look like for us in the future. But it's more than that. I want you to know that I made a promise to you long before you ever knew about a two-by-two."

She struggled to think, it clouded her head with the way he spoke the word, "Baby," to her. She felt the shift in the atmosphere. Could he really want her more than just a best friend, too? Her heart ached with the sweet joy of it.

"Will you wear this promise ring? Will you be my girl?" Tyler took the ring out of the box and held it up to her to accept it. *Please God*, he prayed, *let her be mine.*

She held her hand up to him, still unable to find the words to say to him. As he slipped the ring onto her finger, she reached out to touch his cheek. Victoria traced the line of his strong jaw, and placed her hand along his neck, leaning in closer to him than she had ever dared to before, not face to face. Not like this with a promise between them.

"Every hour of every day, I love you."

"I love you more," he whispered against her lips, then covered her mouth with a slow, long kiss that showed her just how much. His hands found her face, her hair. How he had dreamed of this moment. It was here, and she was his. He would never let her go.

"Ummm…Hmmm"

They both turned and pulled themselves out of the haze that surrounded them to see Abuela standing there with her hands on her hips. The smile on her face let them know that she wasn't the least bit angry or even shocked.

"Come on inside, lovebirds. I think you will want to see this."

"Okay." Tyler's voice cracked a little in embarrassment.

Victoria gathered everything and placed it into the basket. Tyler slipped the ring box back in his pocket and told her the story of how his parents had helped him. She loved to know they accepted her, too. Victoria had always loved his family, the way they joked with one another, but she also knew of their fierce protection. If they helped him with her ring, that meant they would include her in their circle.

Betty Lou led them back to the lab where Father Jacoby and Solomon were busy at work by a cage positioned in the center of the room. When they turned to see who had entered, Father Jacoby pulled the headphones out of his ears and stepped aside. In the cage crouched a demon, a creature was beyond human form. The deformed face slid out of place in a distorted slant, shifting of skeletal bones. On its forehead were crude markings, slashes marked up most of the skin as if they had appeared from the inside out.

Tyler whispered, "The mark of the beast. 666. Dare I ask what is this thing?"

Victoria stepped forward. "Can we save it?"

Dorothy Lamar said, "Look at it, Victoria. Do you think we could have that walking the streets of downtown Asheville, headed for an afternoon spot of tea?"

Tyler said, "Good point. But how did it get like this? Was this part of that family at the campground?"

Abuela said, "The father didn't mention a lost family member. No, they were intact. This pawn of Satan right here was the Messenger."

Betty Lou said, "When you catch a demon that has the visible markings, humor me by calling them the creature features, then it is evidence that a full possession has taken place with no hope for saving any soul. It has long since departed the body. It becomes a shell for the demon to walk the earth."

Solomon said, "I'm hopeful what I'm working on will be ready soon. It'll reverse the possession and recapture the soul of the person, in theory anyway. It's like breaking into the gates of Heaven or Hell and asking the gatekeepers for the soul to take. So, I haven't quite figured out that last stage of the process."

Abuela turned to Solomon. "I understand your compassion, and your ingenuity is beyond compare. That would be a dangerous invention if it fell into the wrong hands. You may scale down on that line of research, and let us worry about how to decipher the Messengers, their secret communication, and the language they have built since the ancients."

Father Jacoby continued. "A Messenger holds a countless number of demons inside, drawing their strength from each one that joins within it. They communicate, feed to take over unsuspecting hosts, while the Messenger continues on for whatever purpose, a mission from a higher ranked demon who tasked them with the assignment to carry out. With it being here in Asheville, with all of us here, I really can't say I believe that's an accident. He's trying to gain information or find us."

Betty Lou said, "They know we're banding back together. They must be close to something and want to ensure we don't thwart their plan. We might need to call the others."

Solomon turned to them and his eyes gleamed with the excitement of a child about to open the larger of the gifts on Christmas morning. "And I intend to find out what the message is."

Father Jacoby stepped aside and went behind a row of sound equipment and computer screens. Without having to place a single probe on the demon itself, they were calculating all of its body readings.

Tyler stood beside him with great interest. "How are you doing all of that?"

He pointed to the readings, and the 3D projection of the creature spun as he knocked it with his hand. Even though this Solomon St. Pierre was of the odd kind, Tyler recognized that he must also be brilliant to create this out of what appeared to be typical soundboards and DJ equipment from a recording studio.

Solomon answered, "By the floor of the cage, by the thermocouple wiring and electrical pulse designs that take the ambient thermometer used by most paranormal investigators to the next level, I guess you would say as the short explanation of it."

Abuela said, "We need you to ask it some questions, Victoria."

"Like an interrogation?" Victoria sized up the creature. "This day is getting more bizarre by the second."

Dorothy Lamar laughed. "Oh, honey. You haven't experienced nothing yet. I can say this life is filled with one jacked up situation after another."

Solomon said, "You are in a controlled environment if you haven't noticed already. The demon will never leave this cage. Sam Jr. has served me well a time or two, and it never fails."

It shrieked in an unknown language, something primal.

Tyler read from the monitors, "It's a mixture of Latin and Hebrew, 'Do you think a cage can stop the separation of the chaff from the wheat?'"

Father Jacoby said, "This Uncle Sam is amazing, Solomon. Do you know what you've created here? It's simple technology, but so genius. When can I get one? I want one!"

Abuela said, "Stop being a child, Jacoby. Let the girl work."

Victoria took a step forward. The demon spat a foul yellow liquid. It bubbled and ran down its chin, pooling at its feet. It puddled it back up in its hands and licked its fingers.

"Who sent you?"

It mocked her in echo.

"Now that was childish and annoying. Answer me. Who sent you?"

It panted, heavier breathing mixed in with noises that couldn't humans couldn't detect as legible, something no one should be able to hear in this life or the next.

Tyler said from behind her, "Keep going."

Victoria could tell that Uncle Sam picked up something.

"Why did you come here? What do you want?"

Multiple voices speaking different languages burst forth from the demon, "We wanted an enemy. Seems we found another one. Another one. Another one. Let me count the enemies and drop them one by one."

She watched as they all moved to the panel, eyes intent on the screen. Victoria wished that she could see what they were looking at. Abuela put her hand to her chest. Dorothy and Betty Lou grabbed for each other and locked arms.

She knew she had to end this. Something wasn't right. Something was building from within the demon, a power was transforming it. She watched as it contracted, writhed, its bones made loud popping sounds as if knuckles cracking against a microphone reverberating on a surround sound speaker system.

"With the power of the Holy Spirit and the Lord, Jesus Christ, I demand you to tell me your name."

His guttural speech, unrecognizable to any human ear, even those trained in demonology or ancient languages would not have been able to decipher the mutterings that came through between the pitter-patter of the breaths, expelling a cloud of chilling breaths with each exhale.

Tyler yelled, "Its name is Nuntius Satanae."

She spoke it with an authority that could only come from one anointed with the gift of the Spirit, to drive out the demons and casts them to hell, "Nuntius Satanae, I cast you into the depths of hell. Leave this Earth to harm no one again, in the name of the Father, the Son, and the Holy Spirit. Amen and amen."

The demon wailed, "No, it is not my time. Master, forgive me. They know not what they do."

"Depart. Speak no more. Begone, in the name of Christ, the Father of all things holy and light."

The demon's body fell limp as if the evil within him had nowhere to go but fold upon itself. It lay crouched on the floor. There were no vapors released, no black smoke billowed out of its mouth. It lay motionless, and Victoria felt a shift in the electrical energy of the room.

It was no longer filled with an ominous presence looming over her like a shadow. All she could feel was the warmth of the light as she joined those behind the panel. Victoria could finally see all they had observed. The looks on all their faces told her they were in something now that could be qualitatively regarded as one of the darkest days they had faced.

"It has chosen a vessel," Father Jacoby shuddered. "The Messenger has revealed to us who it is. In his ignorance, he did not know that Solomon had linguistic experts upload ancient texts. Sanskrit and Tamil, mixed with Latin and Hebrew. There were ancients the Messenger was carrying inside him."

Solomon said, in his unique melodic voice, "The burning is coming, to burn the chaff from the wheat. The time is near, let all souls prepare for the days ahead."

Dorothy said, "It's biblical prophecy."

Tyler ground his fists together. "Well, let's find this vessel and kill it before it's too late. Let's do the same thing to it as we did to this thing, this Messenger. We can send our own message, straight back to hell."

Abuela said, "It's your sister, Victoria. They have chosen Abrianna. She is the vessel."

"Are you serious? Did it say her name?" she questioned. "Show me."

Victoria leaned over the monitors as they rewound the voice recordings.

"There," commanded Father Jacoby. "Stop."

Victoria did not see Abri's name within the translation. "It's not there, Abuela. It's not true."

"Yes, it is, and don't question how I know, child. Just know I do."

Dorothy Lamar said, "He came again? When? Here? Now? Manuel, are you here?"

Abuela shook her head as if clearing the fog. "Just know that Abri is not safe where she is anymore. We knew it was a den of demons stalking halls disguised as an institute for troubled youth."

Tyler took her hand in his and let her know she was not alone in this fight. "Tell her everything this Messenger of Satan said. She needs to know it all."

Betty Lou said, "They've been harvesting souls, creating these creatures, and Lord knows what else there at that hospital. All of this for Abrianna, Victoria, or they wouldn't be here for us. They are looking for Manuel. To stop the exorcist from intervening."

Victoria said, "But Abuelo passed years ago."

"They don't know that, my dear," said Abuela. "When the light is strong, the presence is still felt. Still around us, even now."

Solomon clapped and packed up his equipment. He picked up his earpiece, "Egor, we have a cleanup on aisle three. Cleanup on aisle three."

Solomon grabbed Betty Lou's hand and dropped it through his arm to escort her out of the door, but not how they had come.

He turned as he opened the door, bowed and announced, "Let's all go to the movies."

Abuela rolled her eyes. "We don't have time for these antics. Why does he always have to be so dramatic!"

Father Jacoby said, "You gotta love him."

She pointed at Victoria and Tyler and said, "Love is in the air, all right. Guess what I caught them doing red-handed, or red-tongued if I must be bold."

"Abuela!"

Father Jacoby laughed. "Well, there goes the old saying, don't kiss and tell. Don't kiss in front of your Abuela, children, or she will tell."

Victoria spun the ring around her finger, it seemed so long ago they had their moment on the stone bench in the middle of the butterfly garden. Such a strange life this was turning out to be, as she glanced behind her to see the lifeless form of the creature cold in the cage.

That would be her sister if she didn't hurry. She had a fear that time was running out. God, give me the ability to save her. Give her the strength to fight any demons that come against her. Please bring my sister back and let her still be my sister. Amen.

Light is Stronger

The movie theater room had three rows of red leather, reclining seats. The 3D symbol and the movie glasses sleeves let Victoria know that they might experience a demon movie a little too close for comfort. With a wave of Solomon's hand, the video projected on the giant screen. It surprised Victoria when she saw herself, just minutes before, now as if she was the star in a movie. Except she knew how real it was, her insides were still shaking from it.

Father Jacoby turned around to her and said, "You need to see it all."

"Me watching myself isn't really going to help me much, now, is it?"

Abuela said, "Trust him."

She didn't like to hear her own recordings of herself singing when she and Tyler experimented with his sound equipment and amp system. Seeing herself on the wall screen made her question everything. Was this the way of a true exorcist, or was she just playing some role passed on by her grandfather, not a part meant for her? Would she measure up? Was there even a standard to compare herself to?

Her mind raced to a thousand places all at once. She tried to focus on the closed captioning, reading how the Uncle Sam was picking up all of the low guttural tones indescribable to the human ear, those layers upon layers of strings of sentences hidden behind the panting noises and grunts.

Father Jacoby admired the screen and clapped. "That is truly phenomenal."

Abuela hushed Father Jacoby. "Can you please stop feeding this man's ego for one minute."

Solomon's eyes sparkled in the dark. "It is genius if I say so myself."

Betty Lou snickered. "You say so, all the time, dear."

He shouted, "Pause!"

Victoria's hand found her chest. She was getting jumpier by the minute. Seeing the demon in the cage reminded her of how evil lurked there, waiting to rip out her tongue, her brain, her soul.

Abuela walked towards the projection screen as if she were now playing a professor role. She pointed, standing on her tippy-toes. "Look right there. Do you see that?

Victoria leaned forward. She saw a light shadowing her, almost as if someone had taken a crayon to draw her outline. "What is that?"

"You have just captured the Spirit. Jacoby, look. Manuel would have loved this."

Dorothy Lamar said, "When others see, they will believe. The light is stronger than the darkness, and it is growing in her."

Betty Lou said, "You have to film me next with your new filter system, Solomon. I want to see if I have that glow."

"Nobody's taking any images of me. I don't want all this gray hair to show," said Father Jacoby. "Anyway, back to training. Sometimes exorcisms last hours, days, weeks. What I witnessed with Victoria reminds me more of Manuel's style. Was it his way, a natural gift, or his simple belief that held him? I don't know."

Dorothy Lamar recounted the morning in the forest under the pines to catch Solomon up on the day's events. There was no surveillance video, but she retold it in vivid detail. I'm sure if he had known what was about to occur, he would have sent out video hounds or drones.

Abuela said, "This must explain it. When Jesus conducted exorcisms, there was no verse after verse battles of the demon-possessed being cast from souls. It was a miraculous event, short but sweet for those who released from their bonds. He did so with authority, power from God, and the understanding that what He spoke was life."

Victoria sat back in the seat, thinking of her grandfather's journals. She remembered he would calculate the duration, time frames spanned ranges just as Father Jacoby spoke of.

Tyler said, "Remember Paul's annoyance at the demon-possessed woman following him shouting, and he commanded the devil to come out in the name of Jesus. The Book of Acts recounts it came out that very hour. As with Victoria, she speaks the name of Jesus with innocence, purity of belief. She is sure Christ is real, and the demons flee at the mention of his name when she speaks the way she does."

Father Jacoby said, "The wolf also shall dwell with the lamb. The leopard shall lie down with the young goat. The calf and the young lion and the fatling together and a little child shall lead them."

Abuela whispered, "To have the faith of a child. Us old folks have a lot to learn from you, youngsters. Manuel would have been proud to witness this today."

Dorothy Lamar said, "I want to warn you, though. Now that we've seen this and have evidence of the Spirit strong within her, we can't get this narcissistic boastfulness or pride over it. It's not Victoria. It's not by our own power, but by His might."

Victoria replied, "I knew it could not be me. I am a nobody. I am just a girl who days before this only dreamed of music, fashion, and concert days. I didn't know the Lord. I am nobody special. It has nothing to do with me."

Tyler said, "You are the most specialist girl I know. The specialist! God knew you and called for this purpose. He's equipped you with what you need to battle against the darkness."

All of them turned back to the screen to study the light shining around her, in awe that God sought them all out to do His work, work like this. Abuela's cell phone broke the reverence in the room.

Before she could even glance to see the screen, she frowned. "It's Gideon. How can I explain all of this to an unbeliever?"

Dorothy said, "You wait. The evidence always speaks for itself. We never have to."

Solomon said into his microphone necklace, "Egor, we have cell phone use in the theater. Call management. Let's get her kicked out."

Before she picked up, she snapped. "Oh my God, seriously. You have to be the weirdest man on the planet."

Victoria looked at Tyler. "If it were your parents, would you tell them?"

"They are Christians, raised me in the church all my life, but I don't know how I will even start this conversation with them about Abri. Maybe once we help Abri, it will be the last of this, and no one else will need to know."

"Wouldn't that be nice, dear, but don't bet on it?" Betty Lou said. "There are countless evils in this world. Victoria has a special gift that will forever be put to use if the vision I received is true."

"Vision?" Betty Lou questioned. "You keeping secrets now?"

"Some things are better left unsaid. She is too young to know about her years ahead because as we both know our life events have a way of rewriting what we see."

"What did you see?"

Dorothy said, "I can't believe I let the one-word vision slip. It will now be an endless barrage of my psychic abilities. That's why I've lived a quiet life away from such foolish questions about what I know. Girl, you can't just go around demanding from the ASPs to tell you about future events or even what is happening in five minutes. We aren't starting that game. How about you let it be, sweetheart. It's not bad, that's all I will say."

Victoria kept an eye on Abuela as she steady talked to Gideon. She watched as she pulled on Father Jacoby's sleeve, her face growing pensive by the second.

Finally, she pushed the phone her way. He wants to speak to you.

"Are you having fun with Tyler? I know he was coming up to visit you this weekend."

She looked at Tyler. "Yeah, Papi. We are having lots of fun here in Asheville. A hell of a time, if you want to know the truth. How is Mami?"

"Just wanted you to know I love you."

Tyler crinkled his nose and wagged his finger at her.

She handed the phone back to Abuela. "Well, that was short, and he hung up before telling me how she was doing Someone called out to him but I couldn't make out what they said."

"He was in a hurry," Abuela said. "And we must be as well. Pack your equipment, Solomon, Father Jacoby."

Father Jacoby asked, "What's going on?"

"Gideon Hartwell, that foolish, stubborn man is on his way as we fiddle-faddle around here to pick up Abrianna from Cambion. We all know that he is about to walk into a den of thieves, a pit of hell with no weapons or the Spirit of the Lord. He is going to turn into one of those in the other room or die within seconds of entering the lair."

Victoria cried out, "He has no clue what he's walking into! Why didn't you warn him?"

"I told him the best way I could, but he is a hard-headed lot. He wouldn't listen to me. What do I say as he is driving? Oh, your daughter has a demon? He would wreck or just call me a crazy old fruitcake. Either way, it wouldn't end pretty."

Solomon said, "Egor, get the Sam Sr. ready. We are about to send our little friends on an excursion."

Victoria asked, "Can you please tell me what is going on?"

Abuela grabbed her hand. "We have to get your sister and your father before it is too late for both of them."

Tyler said, "You are right. We have no choice. Remember when we saw the plans of Cambion. It's filled with those things. My concern is how it will all play out. Us against all of them."

"Have no fear," Father Jacoby said. "Abuela and I will be there with you."

Dorothy stepped up. "If you think you're leaving us out of the action, you're out of your blessed mind."

Abuela said, "This is our family. There are sixty-six demons in wait for us when we get there. That is what the Messenger meant by the 66, and we saw the little dots popping on the screen, so I know that's what that fiend was talking about. We can't risk any of your lives."

Betty Lou grabbed Abuela. "You are our family. We are all family, righteous daughters of the King called to one body of Christ. And because you are my sister in Christ that means my granddaughter is taken by a demon, too."

"And nobody messes with our granddaughter," Solomon said. "They don't know who they are dealing with."

Solomon led them out to a hanger. Tyler's voice rose in excitement, "I've ridden in a fire engine red Lamborghini, and now I'm about to ride in a jet?"

"Not quite. You get something better. You get the newer version of the Fat Cow who I have renamed Sam Sr."

Instead of a leer jet or prop plane, a Vietnam era Chinook was waiting for them to board through the cargo loader. Father Jacoby said, "Brings back memories of my chaplain days. Army strong. They called me Sergeant Rock because I stood on the unmovable Rock, the Lord!"

They piled in and found themselves face to face on stadium-style red seats. If Victoria could just close her eyes, she could imagine that she was about to take a ride at the amusement park, and Egor was the ride attendant. Father Jacoby led them in prayer as they begin their ascent into the heavens.

Abuela said, "Cambion will not know who is coming to town. They shall all ask, 'Who are these that fly like a cloud, and like doves to their windows?'"

Father Jacoby said, "Pull out the tracking devices, and we will review the architectural blueprints. Abuela has just given me an idea. See how God uses the Spirit of others to craft the plans that will come to a successful end."

Victoria tried her best to block them all out. She stared down at the ring on her finger. It felt eons away from her and Tyler's time in the garden, and her heart grew anxious. He leaned over and kissed her cheek. A calmness washed over her as they laced their fingers together. She had a light, this glow surrounding her on screen. Victoria would have never believed she was worthy without seeing the proof of it with her eyes.

Tyler broke through her thoughts and started to sing, "This light of mine, I've gotta let it shine …"

One by one, they picked up the tune and started their praise before the battle. With the roar of the Chinook, it was difficult to hear the voices, but she knew they followed along. Victoria sat back and watched them, amazed at how much her capacity for love had grown. It was as Dorothy had said.

They were all family. United under the same cause, under the calling and authority of Christ.

Victoria sang along, "This light of mine, Lord, let us shine, let us shine, let us shine."

She had no doubt that He would let it be so with them all.

Escape Plans

After refueling once, they made it to Cambion Heights with no hyperventilation on Victoria's part. Father Jacoby detailed the plan, which kept her preoccupied and had them repeat it multiple times.

Solomon and Egor were to set up the equipment for the ride home with any safety measures to transport Abrianna if they found her in a state that would be less than hospitable. Dorothy and Betty would keep the front staff busy acting as visitors. Victoria and Tyler would gain entry into the building from the roof. Abuela and Father Jacoby planned to take one of the service entrances and find the nearest supply closet to pull two demons into it at a time to level the playing field.

At any opportunity, they were to silence the demons and their methods of communication. Chopping heads off could stop the transmission through telepathic means. Tyler liked the feel of the Katana in his hands and refused to let it go the entire flight.

It seemed like a perfect plan until Dorothy radioed in from her earpiece. "Gideon is here now. I overhear him demanding that he get his daughter. We are in line behind him. Looks like there will be trouble faster than we expected."

Victoria shimmed down the side wall to the emergency fire escape route with Tyler close behind. "We've got to hurry. If we can extract her, then the sisters can snatch Papi, and this whole nightmare will be over."

Tyler thought, *look at us scaling the wall of a mental hospital like some masked superheroes. Never dared dreamed about this one on the bucket list.*

Victoria scowled, "Why did it have to be on the third floor?"

"Because nothing is easy."

"Apparently not," she grimaced as she bumped her head on the metal bar above her. "This is it, but I'm having a little trouble here."

Tyler tried to open the window, but it would not budge. "No one thought of the locks."

"Not true," Victoria pulled out a glass cutter. "Solomon slipped this in my bag before we left the chopper." As soon as she cut the hole large enough to slide her hand into the latch to unlock it, the smell escaped the room and knocked her in the face.

"Wow. Just you saying chopper sounds sexy. And that outfit. Hmm …"

"Oh, my goodness. Are you trying to flirt while we hang from the side of the building?"

"What? I can't give my woman a compliment?"

"What you can do is give me a hand. Hoist me up. Pull-ups were never my strong suit."

With Tyler's help, Victoria climbed through the window. Abrianna lay lifeless on the hospital bed with tubes coming from every possible place.

"What do we do now? Abuela, she is hooked up to all these machines. It appears she is unconscious." Victoria didn't want to let Abuela know just how grave the situation was, and by the looks of Abri, she was close to it.

Solomon sent out the signal. "Betty Lou, get to the third floor. We need your medical expertise."

Her voice came over the line, "We are kind of in a pickle at the moment, dear. Can't you just figure it out, maybe ask the internet? Solomon, hook into Victoria's phone and talk her through anything she needs help with."

"We don't have time for that," whispered Tyler, afraid to wake up Abrianna out of fear of what he might discover. "Just start pulling the tubes out."

"Are you serious? What if we hurt her?"

Father Jacoby interrupted, his voice crackling on the line, "You have a creature headed your way, just turned down the corridor. It's alone. Take care of it."

Tyler peeked through the door. Far off, the person was normal looking enough, in a business suit no less.

Until it came closer, and that's when Tyler could see the markings of the beast and the cuts across his face as if he had made out with a cheese grater. He closed the door behind him in hopes it would not discover them. Victoria played doctor as Solomon told her how to cut the monitors off without causing the alarms to sound.

"It's just saline," Victoria said in relief.

"How do you know?"

Victoria pointed to the label on the bag. "Solomon said just to release the tubes from the machines. He would stop by someone in the network to pick up medical supplies on our way out of here to last us until we got home if Betty Lou deems it's necessary. Do you think you can carry her?"

She unhooked the last of the sensors from her head and neck. "I think this is all. Be careful with her."

Tyler lifted her up from the bed. "She weighs nothing, look at the bones sticking out. Oh God, Victoria, how did she get like this so fast? I'm scared I will break her, she's so emaciated."

"What do you think you are doing?" The demon at the door stopped their assessment of her condition. The three-piece power suit hid a darker power within. It shrieked, "Get your hands off of him! Room 7, stat!"

Father Jacoby broke into the prayers that were already streaming from Victoria's lips. "They are coming. Masses of them. Do nothing rash until we get there, do you hear me?"

Tyler turned toward the window and called to Solomon on the transmitter. "Can you land on the roof?"

Abrianna stepped toward the devil, without fear. Her sister was safe now they had arrived. "In the power of Jesus' name, I cast you out."

The demon fell to his knees as Tyler hit him with the holy water, burning his eyes. He withered in pain and spat. "This will be a highlight of my life, to kill my very first exorcist. We'll be even because I know how you like to keep score."

She knew he communicated with another demon by the way his head twisted towards the door away from her gaze. He was waiting on backup. Before she could get out the next line of prayers, the room was crawling with a demonic force, unlike anything that Victoria experienced at the campsite.

The family still looked human.

There before her crawled the creature from the cage, multiplied by ten. "Get back!" She held up her crucifix and waved it in front of the demons.

Abuela broke through. "Hurry. Get out of there. What is Tyler doing? Why aren't heads rolling?"

Solomon commanded, "They've got Betty Lou and Dorothy surrounded. Egor, we need you. Go get my woman, now!"

Tyler placed Abrianna back down on the bed like a china doll and drew the Katana. There would be no need for backup. He would just chop his way through the chaos.

Father Jacoby and Abuela made it to the room in time to see the last slice of the neck of the lesser demons as Victoria warded off the commanding presence staring her down in a battle of faith and will.

Father Jacoby asked, "Where did you learn to do that? I could barely drive my car without running off the road at sixteen, much less fight demons?"

"Years of gaming comes in handy. My mom would be proud to see it put to such good use. She always said it was a waste of time."

Abuela said, "Don't exorcise Abri's demon here. She is too weak, Victoria. It could kill her. I've never seen a body in so devastating a shape. Dios mio. Let's go with the plan for Asheville."

They didn't have time to discuss the next steps. The demon toying with Victoria levitated. "Jacoby and the old woman are no one of consequence, I don't even remember your wretched name. That does mean Manuel, my dear old friend, is here, too. Where is that old companion of mine? I would like to catch up."

"Give me my granddaughter back, you fiend. You foul damned soul."

Sirens wailed in the distance. The demon took flight, shot across the room with a force an Olympic medalist could not match and shoved Tyler out of the window. It all happened so fast. Tyler couldn't react, fight back, brace himself. No one could.

Victoria collapsed to her knees by the bed and cried out, "Solomon! Please save Tyler! Oh, God, please save Tyler."

She screamed as more demons piled into the room and climbed up the sides of the wall with disjointed cracking of bone and tearing away of flesh. Demons clung from the light on the ceiling above her head and grabbed her hair while another held on to her legs, ripping into her jeans, cutting her flesh.

Flames danced in the eyes of the one who pushed Tyler as he turned to face them.

Father Jacoby stepped forward, holy water in hand, and flicked at the fiends at Victoria's feet biting into her ankles like dogs. He prayed the Lord's Prayer with Abuela at his side.

The demons' clothes hung from borrowed flesh and were smoldering and burning to shreds from the evil pushing its way to full being. They pounced upon Abuela and Father Jacoby and crawled against their chests. The movement forced them on their backs. With gnarled hands and extended claws, the reptilian devils' faces melted molten lava to reveal the reptilian form beneath the human disguise grabbed Abuela by her hair and yanked her out of the door through the hallway. Victoria shuddered at the screams but was held motionless by fear.

Father Jacoby did all he could to keep the creatures at bay, but they had a firm hold on his body and dragged him by his feet and arms, snapping against him with fanged teeth.

The commanding demon gave the others instructions in a foreign tongue, adjusted his tie as flames leaped from the collar of his dress shirt, and sauntered out of the room confident strides as if he won this fight.

Victoria had no choice. She would die there, along with Abri, her father, Abuela, her new family, and Tyler if she did not take control now. She found her voice and commanded in the name of Jesus that all demons flee. No billows of smoke appeared like a magician trick.

Only crumbled one by one, toppled over like toy soldiers. She held the crucifix on the long chain out from her shirt and placed it on the wrist of the demon still holding her hair. The burn released the hold, and Victoria dropped to her feet, stumbling against the bed.

She swept the room of all demonic force, except the one who threatened to end her life. The coward of a demon spread its black wings and flew through the broken glass into the moonless night, hidden behind fast-moving gray clouds, shielding the world from light.

Which way should she go? After Abuela and Father Jacoby or should she follow through with the window escape plan and do her best to lift Abri herself?

Victoria leaned out of the frame to see if the helicopter was anywhere visible. That's when she saw Tyler barely holding on with one hand to the bottom of the railing. The other was bleeding and unable to grasp the metal bars.

"Oh, thank you, Jesus! Tyler! Please, Tyler. What can I do?"

"Where are the demons? Don't worry about me. Save yourself."

"They're all gone. One just flew away, black wings and all. They've got the others, and we still have Abri in the room. Hold on, Tyler. I will get you."

"Three stories down could make for a hard fall, you better hurry or I'm done-did-dead."

She grabbed his forearm, and with all of the strength she had left, she pulled him up enough to where he could get his body over the railing and on the platform.

She crawled back through the window and to her horror Abrianna was not in bed. "Oh my God, no! Where is she? How did this go so wrong so fast?"

"Baby, we walked into a devil's playground. That Messenger played us, and we thought we gained information from him. He scoped out the team, I guarantee it. Heads have to roll. We can't question anymore, only destroy."

She called for the rest, but the airwaves were quiet. Her family was in jeopardy. "What do we do?"

"Standing here won't solve nothing. We have to move. Father Jacoby must have the tracker, but we have to take our chances."

"No, there it is." Victoria pointed to the corner of the hospital bed.

He grabbed the device along with Abuela's cross. "We have to find them."

He flicked it on and saw the tiny red dots scattered all over the screen like a video game map locator. They fled out of the building like rats through different exits and out of screen view. The sirens grew louder, signaling the Calvary was arriving soon, and the lights were flashing through the glass of the first-floor entryway when they arrived downstairs. This was the last action step in various escape plans if all others were a disaster.

Her first rescue attempt would not be one for the record books. That was for sure.

There were lifeless demons strewn from one corner of the room to the next. Egor stood in the middle of the lobby amongst all the overturned furniture, the place a complete disaster.

Victoria screamed over the sirens, "Where is everyone? Where is my sister?"

Egor pointed toward the main entrance doors, "Solomon has Betty Lou and Dorothy. I'm sorry about what happened, Victoria."

He would say no more. Egor's head dropped in shame, and he refused to look at her. He kicked at the bodies littered on the floor for no reason than to lash out.

Victoria and Tyler turned around and walked down a dark corridor, the banging of each child on a patient door unnerved her. Faces mashed against the barriers, distorted innocent faces still, but evil festering within. Through the glass, they were shrieking and baring teeth, rubbed their hands along the walls and pulled out their hair. One girl held out her hand as an offering to her, and she could see the clumps of stringy hair matted as if not combed for weeks.

Victoria would never tell another soul, but at that moment, she was the most afraid as she had ever been in her entire life. Somewhere Abrianna was barely holding on, and hope was draining fast. The horde of demons still left in the institute had Father Jacoby and Abuela tormented or tortured by this point. Her father was in the middle of this destruction and with no strength or understanding to fight these beasts.

She grabbed Tyler's hand and pulled him into a sprint down the hallways with no plan other than to attack anything that moved and locate those she loved so dear.

He said, "Wait, look at the slower moving dots here. I bet that means that's where Abrianna is, and it looks like they're headed for a back entrance. Come on."

All of his years spent deer hunting with dog trackers and following green dots of tanks on battle maps was coming in handy as he led Victoria through the maze of the treatment facility. As they ran, Victoria refused to look to the right or the left of her because all she could think about were the poor souls of those children locked behind the doors she couldn't save. If she only had time, she would save them all.

With each passing door, she prayed to God, "In the name of Jesus', release these children from their darkness. Cast any unclean spirit out of their precious bodies, and cast them all to hell."

Lord, let that be enough for now. She would have to come back for them, but not today. She had her own to protect if she could find them before it was too late.

Tyler pointed. "It's just up ahead. Are you ready?"

"No. Say a prayer, a verse, anything."

"Put on the whole armor of God, that you may be able to stand against the wiles of the devil."

Abuela screamed when she saw Victoria. Her eyes widened with fear, and she could feel the tingling sensation down her back that told her something was so close to her, something so evil. She could feel its panting against the nape of her neck. Victoria turned sharp and placed the crucifix against the forehead of the demon.

"By the power of the Holy Spirit, depart. In the name of Jesus, I command you to leave this body. Save this soul, Lord."

The creature in the nurse uniform fell to the side, toppled over and lay flat on the dingy floor of an old shipping dock entrance. Black vapor billowed out like puffs of smoke from a chimney but expelled itself from the body.

Tyler checked her pulse and sighed. "She is still breathing. Thank you, God!"

The voices of the demons rose in unison from behind them, echoing down the service hallway, "They are getting away. The Master will punish us. Hurry. We can't let them escape!"

The demons closed in on them. The lights flickered off one by one, and Tyler let out a yell so loud it shook Victoria to the core. He took the holy water out of his side pocket and flung it at the approaching beasts, who dropped to the floor writhing and frothing at the mouth.

Victoria prayed as she pulled on the back of Tyler's t-shirt, "If this woman could be saved from demonic possession here in this pit, there could still be hope for Abrianna. She had no markings, just like this one."

The exit door swung open. Victoria held the crucifix high, her stance strong. Before her prayers could be released, she stood face to face with two police officers. Cars were barricading what appeared to be an ambulance disguised to sneak Abrianna off-site. A little reconnaissance of their own interrupted demon plans.

A circle of police officers protected Abuela, making sure she was fine. They covered Father Jacoby's shoulder with a blanket.

An echo from the megaphone startled her, and she shielded her eyes from the bright lights. "Put down your weapons."

Victoria lowered her arms but clasped the crucifix in her hand. Tyler came to a dead stop behind her, the Katana clanging to the floor.

"There is a woman in there that needs medical attention," he said to the cop nearest him. "And the children. Please help the children."

The cops looked to each other in confusion.

"How many are inside?"

Victoria cried, "Too many."

Father Jacoby stepped over to them. "Abrianna is safe for the moment, but we have to go."

Abuela pointed to Egor pushing Abri in a wheelchair around the corner of the building. "Solomon's waiting for us."

The cops handcuffed two ominous figures, a man and woman, the ones there to transport Abrianna away in the mock ambulance. They seethed with menacing hatred. The woman looked to the man and nodded her head towards Victoria. He was filled with such intense fire Victoria could feel the heat he radiated at a distance. His eyes locked on hers, and he refused to be moved any further.

"Resisting arrest is not another charge you want to add to the list of this monstrosity of a crime scene, Silas. We knew something was wrong with this place."

The other officer said, "Yeah, every time I drove by here on patrols, it would just give me the creeps. The heebie-jeebies."

A cop turned to her. "Miss, are you don't need medical attention? Your legs are gouged."

Victoria nodded. "Where is my father?"

Abuela cried in Father Jacoby's arms. The ordeal had taken its toll on everyone it seemed.

"Are you hurt? Are you okay?" The cop pressed her.

"Where is my Papi?"

Victoria recognized a look of compassion and sadness of the officer. The eyes told it all.

She turned to Abuela. "Did you see Papi?"

"Yes, dear. We carried him out of there."

"Where is he?"

The officer handed her a card with a number on it. "We'll give you more news when we find out his condition. Someone shot him. He is on his way by ambulance to Mercy Hospital."

"Shot! Where? Is he okay?" She felt her body lose balance. "Abuela, where was he shot? Did you see it? Who was it?"

She noticed for the first time that the front of Father Jacoby's shirt. The blood of her father stared at her, and her mind went blank.

Father Jacoby said, "Adoria is on her way to see to your father. We need to get going, Victoria. Tyler help her, please." He then turned to the nearest police officer, "Tell Scottie we owe him big time for this."

"Nice to know the big guy in charge, isn't it," the officer replied.

"Comes in handy a time or two."

She felt herself being led by Tyler and Abuela, but her steps felt foreign to her, planting feet after the other in a robotic churn of movement. Her sister, filled with an ancient demon, was waiting on her in the Chinook. By the look on the cop's face, her father was fighting for his life.

Abuela whispered, "Let's pray."

Victoria remained quiet, and let them take over the prayers for the time being. The chopper roared to life as they climbed inside. Abri, secured into the wheelchair, her hands, and feet bound with restraining straps as Egor positioned himself between them, was finally awake, but was she? Blank, expressionless eyes flitted between them, and her tongue protruded like a snake as if to smell out her prey close at hand.

Victoria leaned back and studied all of their faces filled with sorrow. There was no singing on the ride home. No breaks as they stopped for gas. No questions asked as Betty Lou kept watch over Abri's vital signs.

The only sounds heard through the loud reverberating turbine engines were the pantings of the demon inside Abri as it taunted, "I will separate the chaff from the wheat. I will make them all burn, burn, burn. And you, my sister, will be the first to go, at the rising of the sun."

Take Me

buela tried her best to take another call from Adoria, but at 15,000 feet, the connection could be sketchy at best. She wouldn't have been able to hear her voice even if she caught her because of the loud roaring noises that reverberated on and on.

Instead, through the constant barrage of text messages, Victoria learned that her father's condition was critical.

They would land any minute. Could Victoria even will her body to move from the chopper? Her body, brain, everything about her felt numb. She looked at the frame of her sister once so vibrant and full of life and realized she was more like the ghost in the forest, lost. Was she fighting to find the light?

Abuela patted her hand. "You can't cast it out now. She's too weak. I fear it will kill her if we try. We need more time."

Tyler tried his best to reassure her. "I know it's all gonna work out. This is happening for a reason. Just have faith."

Victoria said, "That's easier for you to say. That's not your father we left behind shot in a hospital. Would you be with me right now or him?"

He said, "I would want to cast every single demon back to hell I could lay my hands on so they're no longer attached to this Earth. Where they can't hurt another soul again, by demonic possession or bullets. That's what I'd be doing right now."

Abuela said, "When we fight, we fight for all the future souls that could've been taken. We set the future people free, and they never knew their day was coming and wouldn't believe us even if we told them. We rid Massachusetts of many demons in that one sweep attack tonight."

Solomon said, "By the sword, we seek peace, but peace only under liberty. That's the state motto. How ironic."

"And how does he know these random facts?" Tyler asked.

Betty Lou said, "He searches everything, like your name, for instance, he knows what that stands for, too. Ask him."

Solomon said, "Your name means gatekeeper. It's perfect for your prayer protection duties. In fact, I think it fits nicely for my next project. I might recruit you for the tech business. I've always dreamed of having a young protegee to learn my ways so that our technology could carry on and be put to good use."

Dorothy added, "Let's make him a golden ticket, and he can win a prize to inherit your freak show."

Tyler said, "Sounds like a plan. And I've got my tattoo idea, a bear busting out of a gate."

Victoria couldn't help but feel a weak smile form. "Wearing a cross and throwing holy water?"

"See, that's why I love you. You give my thoughts deeper meaning. You complete me."

Abuela said, "So, now the lovebirds are speaking adoration. Just proves the power of suggestion."

Victoria turned to Abri. Her sister had no faith in a higher power, nothing that stitched her soul to the understanding of grace. They were an unlikely pair, demon and demon hunter. It could have very well been Victoria strapped to the chair. That realization hit her hard. If they were after the granddaughters of Manuel Ortega, then what plans did they have for her next?

Did the beasts choose her because she was the youngest? Because she didn't have a Tyler by her side? Abri had such a tough year, the whole cyberbullying craze was just getting ridiculously stupid. Was she so emotionally weak that it targeted her?

How could Abrianna stand against this demon?

"I know what you're thinking," said Dorothy. "She's a fighter. Look at her. If this has been going on for six months and she hasn't been taken over by possession and the soul-killing, then she is stronger than you think." She patted Victoria on the knee. "You, my dear, are stronger than you think."

Victoria felt far from strong. Her own determination felt lacking. With every look around her, she would catch a glimpse of the blood on Father Jacoby. No matter how she tried to steady her heart, it would not catch the rhythm. Her mind replayed the events of the day. The horrors. The voices of the demons more chilling on repeat than in the moment since the adrenaline had worn off.

Victoria was so afraid to even whisper a prayer Abrianna's way in fear it would cause her last heartbeat. She appeared that frail. Her once bright skin stretched across the bones of her face, her eyes sunken into shadows, and sallow patches marked a pallor close to the tomb.

Abuela said, "Thank God your father didn't see her condition. Was she like this when you came to me two weeks ago?"

Victoria forced back the tears. "Not like this. The smell, the breathing, the multiple voices, yes. But nothing like this. What did you tell Mami?"

"She knows we've taken Abrianna back with us. I told her the treatment facility wasn't on the up and up, the director was arrested, and we were on our way back to Asheville to provide Abrianna the help she needs. Adoria took the first flight out of Raleigh to go to Gideon. She'll be reporting to us, with no need to know what we're about to do here."

Tyler asked, "What do we do, Father Jacoby?"

"We pray as always. We tread soft into this night knowing what is at stake. Even though this poor child's life is on the line, know this, Victoria, the power of Jesus Christ can bring the dead to life."

They filed out of the Chinook. Egor had his instructions to take Abri to the laboratory. One demon in a cage replaced by another. Would they tie her down or make her comfortable as if she were holding on to her last breaths from a terminal illness? Solomon and Father Jacoby carried all the supplies. Abuela linked arms with the sisters. Victoria let them all pass her as she took her place in the back of the procession.

Tyler asked, "What's wrong, baby?"

"I think I need to go to the garden to pray," she whispered. "Alone."

"Even Jesus' disciples went with him to stand watch."

"Didn't they fall asleep?"

"Remember, I'm the gatekeeper. I can stay awake."

They walked in silence. That's all she needed. Not a single word would help her calm down, to heal, to forgive those demons who had torn her family apart. His presence was enough to prove once again that she didn't have the face this by herself.

Earlier as they walked down the French garden trail, she noticed all of the twinkle lights that wrapped the birdhouses, the trees, with the lanterns as indicators that this walk would be well-lit tonight. She thought it was more beautiful now than when she took the path with Tyler under the sun. Her insides screamed of division, beauty, and pain, death and life. Heart. Soul. Darkness. Light.

The bells struck three a.m., yet Victoria wasn't the least bit sleepy, more emotionally exhausted, but not to the point of desiring rest. If she closed her eyes now, all she could see was the blood. She pulled out Abuelo's Bible from her bag. She hadn't picked it up since she and Tyler read the Gospels.

I'm crashing, God. What gets me from this breaking point?

Victoria found the closest bench trellis and propped the Bible open on her lap. She read, "For every man shall bear his own burden."

If her father died, that would leave them to tend to their mother alone, who was so far removed from them, even before the evil struck and cut the cords of normalcy. She laid in the bed half of the time, her father making excuses for her and overcompensated for her like.

He tried so hard, she thought, it's so not fair. It should have been her instead, not him in a hospital room. As soon as the thought formed the sentence in her head, an immediate regret flooded every part of her soul. She didn't mean it. What was wrong with her? Why were her thoughts filled with such despair?

Tears fell. She let them. Victoria couldn't have controlled them if she tried. She was so angry, and the pent-up frustration released itself at once. She felt the scream rise in her throat before she could stop it.

She would have continued her screams, but the shock of what stood before her stole all ability of her voice registry.

"I like this new side of you, keep going."

Victoria recognized he was the demon from the treatment facility, from Abrianna's room. The fiend who almost killed Tyler. Her anger rose, and vengeance coursed through her. Had he been the one who shot her father?

"I will find pleasure in killing you."

"And that is why you will fail," he answered, throwing back his head in laughter that caught wind of a thousand voices. "You are such a fool. All of you that walk this Earth think you can control the darkness? Like you have power over the ancient ones. I am Egypt. I am Samaria. I am the death of you at the rising of the sun. Only fallen angels have dominion over this land, no power in your Spirit but a spark to be crushed at my feet. Soon enough the One will be reborn and take his seat at the right hand of the Master Administrator, Satan of old, the serpent. And we will all rise in true form to bring terror to the light and burn what you see to the ground. Rebirth from fire and destruction. Evil will rise and rule."

As he spoke, Victoria slid her hand inside her bag. She needed her weapon, the crucifix. She was a fool for removing her earpiece and hoped they could hear in the lab.

Victoria whispered, trying to mask the fear in her voice. "Why are you here?"

His charcoal wings glowed red embers like a dying flame aglow. The tail of a snake came into view, whipped around his legs and stretched out long to taunt her. "Don't you know? I am here to kill you and take the vessel back with me."

She caught Tyler approaching over the demon's shoulder, but her reverted eyes were a mistake because it caused him to turn. He hunched his shoulders as if ready to attack, then when he saw Tyler, relaxed as if he did not fear them.

His clawed hand circled Tyler's throat. He lifted him off of the ground and hovered with him, as Tyler's legs kicked under him as if trying to break free. "You alive, boy? What an oversight on my part.

No window to throw you out of this time. How about I just snap your neck."

"And we will not let you escape this time," commanded a voice that stepped from the shadows of the garden. Father Jacoby stood firm, and his eyes lit with fire as he faced the demon. She felt rage consume Father Jacoby, and Victoria could feel the negativity building in the air on the verge of combustion.

"This time. Do you mean your fiasco this evening or ten years ago? We are about to celebrate our anniversary, Jacoby. Let me check my calendar to be sure."

"September 15, 2007. A day I will never forget."

"My legions saw to that, and of course, we succeeded. Just as we will be triumphant tonight."

Abuela appeared. "Victoria, cast him out now. Do not engage in a conversation with a demon, especially this monstrous instrument of Satan."

The demon lessened his hold on Tyler and turned his attention to Father Jacoby. "Think smart, Jacoby. If the little girl casts me out, I can't bring Samuel back to you. Don't you want your Sam back? Who is she to you, anyway? Who is Sam to you, Jacoby?"

"What is he talking about?" questioned Victoria, "We can get new gadgets. I'm sure Solomon has enough Sam's to spare."

Abuela stepped forward. "He's lying to you. Don't listen to this viper. Jacoby, he is the father of all lies."

"Father! Father Jacoby! Father! Daddy! Save me." His voice turned childlike, laced with an innocence that Victoria knew broke the spirit of Father Jacoby. She watched as the fight left his body, and his head hung in overwhelming grief.

As Father Jacoby faded, Victoria felt her Spirit rise up. "Shut up! Don't listen to him, Father Jacoby. In the name of Jesus Christ, I…"

"Stop!" Father Jacoby rushed between her and the demon as if he would be the human shield that would take the casting. "Is he alive? Tell me! Where is he? Where is he? Please!"

"Jacoby! He lies!"

"Why would we kill a pawn so precious? I believe it has become the Master's favorite pastime, to torture his soul, a'pricking him with needles. A'pricking him with pain. And all the day is coming when our torment will reign. A constant pain that never ceases once you start the prick, prick, prick." He flicked his fingernails across Jacob's cheek.

Blood seeped from the scratches, but Father Jacoby did not flinch. Instead, he fell to his knees, and Victoria stepped forward once more. She didn't care what was going on, she'd had enough.

She placed her hand on Father Jacoby's shoulder and felt a cold chill run up her arm. "Whatever is happening here, we can make it stop now. Let me do my job."

"I will give my life for Samuel. Take me instead. Take me."

Abuela screamed, "No! What is your name demon? Speak it now, I command you in the name of Jesus."

"What is your name?" repeated Victoria! She raised her crucifix, "En el nombre de Cristo, libranos del mal."

The demon's wings shook with rage. His visage weakened. Tyler pulled the holy water from his pocket and the blessed water struck the entity in the face, bubbling chaos across the face of the hated one. Father Jacoby fell face first on the pebbles and rock, another gash, this time across his forehead. The demon took flight once more, vanishing against the night.

"Oh, my God!" Victoria screamed as she watched the signs reveal the stage of oppression, and they were all unaware. They had a demon walking amongst them, one of their very own. For how long? For what purpose? The vapor poured like a thin line from his opened mouth and nostrils, swirling up into the night and disappearing in the darkness.

Abuela rushed to him. "Jacoby, please! Please, be alive. I can't lose you, too."

There was no doubt to Victoria that at that moment Abuela loved Jacoby. It was in the way she cradled him in her arms and wiped the blood from his face with the hem of her dress.

Victoria cried one last time. "Demons, leave this place. I cast you back into hell."

Father Jacoby cried in a hoarse whisper, "No, I was so close. He was telling me where my boy was. He was telling me where my boy was! Oh, God, please bring it back. I was so close. Oh, God."

Victoria said, "What is Father Jacoby talking about? Why would he have given his soul just now? Who is Sam?"

"Samuel Wethington," Abuela spoke through tears. "He is Jacoby's son."

Parlor Tricks

Victoria tried to let it sink in, but the enormity of it was almost impossible to fathom. Father Jacoby? A priest? A son? She turned the metal crucifix over and reread the date, September 15, 2007. What other secrets did this date hold? Did Abuela and Jacoby have an affair? Could Sam be their child?

The cut on Father Jacoby's forehead caused blood to pour into his eye. It required stitches and looked as if he'd been in one brutal round with an MMA lightweight champ.

Abuela said, "Betty Lou, we need you."

Victoria forgot about the earpiece communicators. She grabbed hers and secured it.

"Again, busy. Handle it your own self. I've got a company of scoundrels."

"We just left the leader of the pack, and you missed one hell of a garden party."

"I've got our own soiree in the living room. Care to join me?"

Victoria quickened her pace. "What now? Can I just save my sister? That's all I ask!"

Tyler said, "Remember, nothing is ever easy."

"Are you going to remind me that every single time we get into a situation? That will totally get on my last nerve."

"Point taken. Retraction. No getting on Victoria's nerves."

Victoria said, "Father Jacoby is in no condition to fight. Hide him, now. Don't follow us. In the state he is in, he'll just move from oppression, or I fear full possession with another attack."

Abuela conceded and took him to the gazebo instead. Victoria reached for Tyler's hand. "Promise me, you won't let me go."

"Baby, that's not going to happen."

"I need you every hour."

"Every hour of every day."

She realized this would be the fourth time they'd come face to face with evil. Maybe after tonight, she wouldn't have to keep count.

He opened up the patio door. "After you, my dear."

Victoria said, "I think we should establish a rule. You get the holy water in position, and you always go first."

He wrinkled his nose up at her. "If I must." Tyler stepped into the darkened house he'd only gone through a couple of times. The noises clashed like cymbals. Victoria realized the demons had followed them to come to reclaim her sister, and she prayed they'd kept her hidden in the lab. No one could find that secret room unless they knew the layout of the place.

She would push back the powers of darkness and defeat whatever had threatened her family, and now Tyler. A clock chimed in the hallway and reminded her time wouldn't stop for her. It wouldn't bend so she could gain her faith in the full force to cast them to hell on command. Time wouldn't be patient with her and keep the demons sitting pretty and patient as she waited to get ready.

This wasn't a date.

With a jolt to her system, she detected the horrific invisible forces before she found them. They were hungry. Strong.

"Say anything. A verse."

"I love you." He leaned forward to kiss her on the lips. "Just in case something happens in there."

"Nothing will take you away from me, Tyler."

"You just inserted the change into my Bible jukebox to find you a verse, my love," he said. "For I am persuaded, that neither death nor life, nor angels, nor principalities, nor powers, nor things present, nor things to come, nor height, nor depth, nor any other creature, shall be able to separate us from the love of God, which is in Christ Jesus our Lord."

Tyler put his arm around her waist as they stepped through the threshold. They scanned the room, and it was in shambles. The chandelier was the crash they must've heard as it fell. Candles reflected on the teardrops, causing the middle of the room to appear like a campfire illuminating from the fireplace mantle. The mansion would have caught fire if the candles were positioned on any of the moveable pieces because every chest and side table was overturned.

Victoria grew light-headed as a gush of wind swept past her. "What was that?"

"I felt it, too."

They stepped further into the room. Tyler kept pushing furniture out of the way, trying to upright the wrong that had happened there.

"Is anyone in here?"

Behind the overturned settee, Victoria found Betty Lou crouched, her arm extended as she held the crucifix for dear life. Her white hair, which was always pulled back in an elegant twist, was disheveled. Victoria touched her on the shoulder with a light hand as to not scare her, and it still made her jump.

"Is it gone?"

Victoria reassured her. "I don't see anything."

"It was here, and then it wasn't."

Tyler asked, "What was it?"

"A demon. Deceptive and cunning, I perceived that for sure. He wore a tailored suit and would easily pass for a mortal. He could've stepped right off a cover of a magazine but his face was a mighty rage, almost as if he would burst me into flames by looking at his dark eyes."

She only had a glimpse of the man that slid into the back of the patrol car at the treatment facility, but she knew it was him.

Tyler helped Betty Lou to her feet, and she at once went to work to gather her hair back in place. Victoria watched as her fragile hands shook as she fastened the pins.

"Let me help you." Victoria did her best to place them how she remembered Betty Lou's butterfly clasps to be. Victoria kissed her on the cheek. The softness collapsed in a fold of wrinkled skin. "We are here now. It's gonna be alright."

"He was too strong for me alone. Dorothy is with the others. I just came up to take my medication, and this blast, this force, it dragged me in here. I saw nothing, but I could feel the hands on me. Then, he came and spoke death on the wind. When you showed up, it disappeared." She rubbed up and down her arms where bruises appeared, and they came in purplish threes. "Sorry, I'm so shaken up. I'm usually the strong one. Don't tell the others, okay. Especially Solomon."

Tyler said, "As I've learned over the past few days, we all have our moments. A breaking point. We just can't stay with it or I fear we may become one of the things we fight against."

Solomon broke through the earpiece. "Baby, I heard everything. You never have to hide your fear from me. Come and find me, my love. I will comfort you."

She moaned. "Great, my husband's little inventions are at it again. In my panic, I forgot it was there. I can't keep anything from that man."

"As you shouldn't. You are my partner."

"Speaking of a partner, sorry sis."

Betty Lou reassured her over the airwaves. "There was nothing you could've done. He's a strong beast, this devilish fiend. When that entity came my way, he carried demonic forces beyond my experience."

Tyler waited by the door, and his head leaned back against the frame with his eyes closed. The day wore on them all, a slow chip away of energy with each episodic event.

Disorientation dazed Victoria, her senses became a cloudy haze, and she had the suspicion whatever the beings were that attacked Betty Lou might have been out of sight, but they were present in the room with them still.

Victoria murmured as she walked by Tyler, "We need the others."

Tyler's voice dripped with emotion. "Are you okay?"

Victoria nodded toward the area by the fireplace and whispered, "Something is in here with us, evil lurking in shadows."

"Seal the door," Betty Lou commanded. "Do it."

Tyler said, "I don't understand. What am I supposed to do?"

She sighed. "I don't have my sage with me. Place the oil you carry along the doorframes in the sign of the cross. That should keep the entity trapped, at least until we can get the proper equipment to see what is slinking around in here."

Shadows passed along the wall. A vase spoke the presence as Tyler made the sign of the cross on the wooden frames. The shattering was not from a drop on the floor, it was more of an explosion of a stationary object. Windows formed icy, frost crystals from the temperature change. The antiqued wallpaper peeled in the section closest to the window. They said prayers, and the oil anointed the only exit. All three backed their way out into the hallway.

Betty Lou mumbled, "Why did Dorothy Lamar have to be the psychic between us? It's hard to fight something you can't see."

One thing Victoria realized was that demons were deceptive fiends who took pleasure in trickery and mocking those deepest, darkest fears within those it faced.

Tyler put a protective arm around Betty Lou, guiding her down the hallway until she gained a better footing. Victoria had never met someone so honest and genuine, with thoughts on higher places. She watched as Tyler cared for Betty Lou, making her laugh at something ridiculous he must have said. He said nothing was easy, but loving him was the easiest thing she ever figured she would do.

Victoria could tell Betty Lou still needed support how her body hunched forward. Their steps slowed to allow her to catch her breath.

"You two make a sweet couple. One day I want to hear all about how you two met."

Tyler chuckled. "I don't think I'll mind telling that story."

"He exaggerates, Betty Lou. Get used to his story on how I drew on the walls first. I think his memory might be a little vague on who supplied the crayons."

She swirled the promise ring around her finger and liked the way it felt. Solomon made his way toward them and took Betty Lou in his arms, their cheeks resting against each other. The sight of them reassured her that love like hers and Tyler's could withstand whatever they had to face. In the next room. Tomorrow. The day after the next. She saw proof right in front of her.

"Is that going to be us one day?"

He leaned closer to her and kissed her. "Without a doubt."

No doubts. No fears. The Lord was going to be with them on the journey. She had accepted nothing about this would be easy except her love for him, and that would have to be enough for her. But would her faith be enough to take care of Abri and rid the house of the threats against them? Now, that she was not so certain.

Never Lose Hope

doria practiced her floating away method. The purpose was to remove herself from any environmental stimuli that caused her undue stress. Gideon sprawled lifeless on the bed. Blood splattered on his neck and face like a newly painted room brushed by a child.

She visualized herself walking into the artwork on the wall lakeside. A boat rocked against the pier, knocking with a thud, thud, thud. She focused on the repetitive sounds of wood against the post, not the beeping of the machines and the loud pumping sound of the respirator. Adoria curled her toes, grass tickled her bare feet. Honeysuckles perfumed the sweet places where Death was uninvited.

Adoria was alone, isolated even in artwork.

"Oh, Gideon." She leaned against the bed and placed her cheek against his arm. "I love you, old man."

Adoria imagined him ruffling her blond curls, messaging her head.

She wanted to tell him how she was so thankful that he had delivered their baby from the grips of some scandalous criminals. Even when she didn't deserve it, he saved her from herself so many times.

"Wake up and be okay," she whispered. "I've so much to say."

But the only response she heard was the thud, thud, thud of the boat knocking against the pier. No other noises allowed to take rental space within her head. Her body rocked back and forth, feeling the lapping of the water against her pants legs. A wet stream seeped on her leg. Her feet sloshed at a puddle.

Adoria was no longer in the hospital room or beside her husband of eighteen years. Their anniversary was two months away. No, no. She wouldn't think of those things. She was inside the artwork, basking in the sun by the lake. Acrylics pooled on her tongue and was better than regret. It was a lie where she was nonexistent, but nothing could hurt her there either.

She might just stay.

****

Abuela sat under the gazebo with Jacoby. On another night, leisure conversation about the past reminded her that every scar she wore came from a place of struggle but partnered with great love.

Instead, she had to pull the evil seed from its root. Before it tilled deeper to overtake a rotted garden. A wasteland.

"What in the hell were you thinking? Look at you."

Blood poured profusely from the open wound. "Can you figure out a way to stitch me up, please?"

"Betty Lou, get your butt out here. This man is bleeding on the gazebo."

"Hold on. Let me grab my bag."

"Jacoby, not to say this flippant, but what possessed you? Your soul? Did you welcome that fiend? What caused you to do such a desperate thing as damn yourself to hell? How long have you had the infestation?"

"I'm back. See. Pinch me." He muttered, "Can you drop it?"

"Thanks to Victoria. That demon was a master of deception, tricking you into believing they'd give you Sam's whereabouts."

"I had to try. That's why I want a translator and tracker of Solomon's. We can get them talking at least. We can trap one more, and with their network of communication, the location could show where they have Sam held captive."

"It's been ten years. He was just a boy."

Father Jacoby's voice rose with such passion. "I know what you think, Adelita, but you are wrong. Sam is alive. I'll do whatever it takes to bring him back to us. He needs to be here with me. I can't imagine what pain they have caused my innocent child."

Adelita counted the time passed. "He's near Tyler's age."

"Seventeen."

Betty Lou stepped out to the patio and called, "Any hullabaloo's out here?"

"Only Jacoby."

His eyes narrowed. "Enough already."

"You will not live this one down."

Adelita helped Betty Lou step up into the gazebo. She watched as her dear friend winced back in pain from being touched.

She scoffed. "Y'all out here having a grand old time when I'm in there with unseen forces, leaving me all helpless like a rag doll on the floor?"

Jacoby said, "That might've been me attacking one of you a few days more. Help my unbelief."

"It's not that you don't believe, Jacoby. Ask for the right things, and you shall receive, Lord willing."

"Give me my son back. Better?"

Betty Lou looked at him with wise, soft eyes. "Solomon has never given up hope. He works on Sam's behalf. You know why he called all of his equipment Sam?"

Adelita chuckled. "Because he is an eccentric old man that is losing his wide expanse of vocabulary?"

"No." She swatted at Abuela's thigh. "You know he is a top distributor of paranormal technology. By naming it Sam, everyone that discusses their work speaks the names of the gadgets. It's a way for him to send out beacons, a lighthouse calling Samuel back home to us."

Adelita's eyes misted. "I love to pick at old Solomon St. Pierre, but he's always had the biggest heart."

Father Jacoby turned away. "Thank you for that, for never ceasing to have faith."

"He might be your son, but he is our family. Trust he will make his way home."

Adelita said, "It's not impossible. You did."

"Done," Betty Lou announced as she closed up the last stitch. "Jacoby. I'm sure the headache will follow soon enough."

"It's here."

Jacoby tried to stand but still felt so weak, and his legs buckled under him. The wooden planks creaked with their weight.

Betty Lou said, "You aren't up to anymore fighting tonight, and I'm not up to going back inside that house."

Adelita agreed. "Both of you stay here and keep each other company. I will take care of my granddaughter."

"Something else besides Abrianna is in there. It scared me close to death."

Adelita watched her shudder. The sisters had many paranormal experiences in their lifetimes, but she knew that nothing had affected Betty Lou as whatever it was she encountered.

"Will you pray with me, Father Jacoby?"

"Of course."

"You mean if you can?"

"Even the demons believe this and tremble with fear."

Adelita warned. "No more jokes. Now, I'm getting the heebie-jeebies. Are you sure you don't need me to stay?"

"Trust me, I'm okay."

It baffled her for someone she took as a holy man of God, the smoke rose and released from him like the others. Something sent those demons with one mission in mind, to use her granddaughter as a vessel and Jacoby a servant.

When someone shared supernatural, unexplained phenomena together, they forged a special connection. Conversations where no other human being could ever believe what was happening unless they too were part of the experience. Jacoby had a soul bond with his son. Paired with knowing he disappeared from his grasp, that must be what drove him to beg the demon to take him for just a chance to make it right again.

She prayed as she entered the house, her cross necklace raised in front of her. "Send your angel armies before me and encamp them around my granddaughter. Bring her back and destroy every spiritual and physical weapon formed against us. Amen."

She heard the voice of a televangelist and claps echoed in her ears, "Amen and hallelujah, sister."

Out from the shadows of the hallway, from a room that Adelita had never explored, stepped forth a villain in pure form.

She spoke to the team in the earpiece, "Any free demon hunters? I have one cornered so you need to come quick."

It laughed. "You still think you have power over me?"

"Egor included."

"Who has been making a mess in my house now? Am I running a daycare?"

She knew whatever happened to Betty Lou could happen to her if she tried to take on this demon and his legions alone.

She watched as they made their way to her, Victoria led them, Tyler by her side and she felt a surge of pride for them, and joy they would love a little longer than she had.

Solomon held a contraption and swung it in the air. "It's time to burn this fiend back to hell."

Tyler said, "He gets the flamethrower. I get the tracker. Makes no sense, I tell ya."

"And the children shall lead them," Dorothy Lamar proclaimed. "Adelita? Are you okay? Where did it go?"

Her eyes reverted to the next room. "He vanished."

Solomon pointed to the sign that appeared to be from an early 20th century fair. "How fitting. It went into my House of Mirrors."

Tyler said, "Mirrors from an old-school carnival? Can you please tell me why you have this room?"

"Because I thought it'd be fun."

Victoria said, "Well, have the time of your life then. I'm staying right here. Bring out the demon. I'll serve as security in the hallway."

Dorothy Lamar challenged. "You cast demons, and mirrors got you jumpy?"

Tyler told them, "She got stuck in a corn maze late into the night. They had to send out drones to find her and search dogs. It might not be a safe place for her to have her wits about her."

Solomon reassured her. "Position yourself in the middle of us, Victoria. The key is not to get separated. I know the way. I designed the blessed thing, and if all else fails, Egor can shatter the glass."

"And nobody will leave me?"

Tyler said, "Not a chance. Is staying together the idea?"

That seemed like a plan, but nothing was easy, and every attempt so far failed or changed a dramatic course in the opposite direction.

Solomon said, "That's strange."

Betty Lou put her hands on his shoulders, "What now?"

"The lights aren't working. Someone killed the power, but not in the rest of the house."

"Someone or something?" said Jacoby. "I can smell its stench from here."

Adoria whispered, "Who is first?"

All heads turned to Tyler.

"Me?"

"And so, the child shall…"

"Lead them. You've quoted it a time or two, especially when it's convenient for you." He took holy water from Solomon, who had a fanny pack strapped to his side.

Tyler said, "Can I get me one of those?"

Victoria replied, "That screams band leader for sure, Tyler."

"I could keep my lucky picks in there and…"

Betty Lou interrupted, "This battle has raged on long enough, and it's time we take its sinister hold and cast it before it does more harm. Let's be the one to trap this evil trickster and damn him back to hell."

Victoria pushed Tyler forward, staying nestled between them. "I believe in you. Go for it."

"I'm glad you do, baby. That's what I need to here in desperate times. Onward Christian soldiers, let's march into this war."

Tyler led them and sang the lyrics as they inched inside,

"At the sign of triumph

Satan's host doth flee;

On, then, Christian soldiers,

On to victory.

Hell's foundations quiver
At the shout of praise;
Brothers, lift your voices,
Loud your anthems raise."

The Looking Glass

This is the house of mirrors, where souls come to die, thought Victoria as she stepped into the carnival. The mirrors were at least ten feet tall, positioned at odd protruding angles, throwing off even those with the keenest of senses. The clip, clop of Dorothy's boots tapped the hardwood as they inched their way in, marking their position to whatever lurked. With each antiqued column passed, Victoria touched the pine wood and imagined this was an elaborate game of trickery against her. Devils in costumes, a cosplay event come to town.

If only it were true.

A beast flashed in a mirror. Victoria struggled to convince herself it was only a shadow or her vision played tricks on her. The shrillness of the laughter surprised her. A sharp clanging of cymbals. Tyler swayed on his feet as he covered his ears. It was an echoing, deafening experience.

Victoria said, "This is a trap. It's just toying with us."

Solomon replied, "I agree with you, but if they think they can win their game, we have to show them who's the boss."

"But what's the point?" asked Tyler. "Haven't you seen too many of the movies you collect where people put themselves in dumb situations, and it never turns out right?"

"Seen them. No big deal. We've got this." Solomon puffed up his shoulders and extended his contraption. "I ain't afraid of no demon, not with this."

For Victoria, the farther she drew herself from the exit, the more her anxiety levels rose. Fear crept along her arms like vines.

Tyler held up the radar transmitter so that Solomon could catch the demon's location, but when they showed up, the evil was nowhere, despite the menacing screams. The cold crept through as if an air duct had turned on right above them. Everyone shivered as if immersed in ice water.

Victoria doubted. "This is not real. It's a diversion."

Dorothy agreed. "Turn back, Solomon. This doesn't feel right. Betty Lou and Jacoby are out back. It's separating us."

"No, you aren't getting rid of me that easy. We're here," said Betty Lou. "I just needed prayer a few minutes to get my mind to play right at this game. I couldn't leave y'all in here alone. Besides, it's payback time for that joker trying to laugh at me."

Victoria turned. "They want Abri, right? Trapped in here gives them time to find her."

Solomon grabbed her arm as she took a right turn. "This way. And trust me, she's in the securest room of the mansion. Besides, if we don't sweep the house of these fiends now, they will just attack us at every turn. What's the point of saving Abrianna to give her weakened spirit right back to them again?"

When they took the next turn, Egor broke apart a voice recorder with his size thirteen shoe. They were the carnival clowns.

Tyler questioned, "Are we going the right way?" He looked at the screen. The tracker showed dots positioned throughout the maze now, and they appeared to be materializing at a frantic speed. "I think Sam's broke."

"Sam's in perfect condition. My equipment is impeccable in performance." Solomon huffed. "Let me see it."

He showed it to Dorothy, and she grumbled, "One is coming at us now. Let us be still."

Tyler moved closer to Victoria and put his arm around her waist. His lips brushed her hair. "These are what frightened Betty Lou. Not demons just lost souls."

Victoria spoke, "Angry ones if they are working for this demonic crew. Not Casper. I'm not too schooled in the paranormal department, but there's a difference."

As the dot drew closer on the screen, there was nothing before them but mirror after mirror, no visible sign that the dot represented a form. Solomon pulled around the flamethrower positioned on his shoulder and ignited it.

The frame of the demon was clear through the flames. It withered and hissed. "Kill them. Kill them all."

Tyler said, "Not ghosts. I was wrong. Invisible demons."

Betty Lou said, "Good quality, young man. Admitting when you've made a mistake is the first step of figuring out how to make it right."

Dorothy snapped, "Giving a moral lesson in the middle of a demon-infested mirror room? It would be my sis. We've got time for that over tea later."

They watched as the patterns of the dots formed a line like fire ants marching to a picnic.

Victoria held out her crucifix to the invisible forces of darkness. "In the name of Jesus' Christ, with the power of the Holy Spirit, I cast you out, demons"

Tyler said, "Victoria, be careful. There are so many."

Betty Lou said, "Light em' up, Rambo."

The devils writhed outstretched claws, pawing at the space between them. They were snarling, fanged teeth in elasticized jaws of serpents spread wide, threatened and bracing to strike.

The shrieks lessened with intensity. Solomon cut off the flamethrower. The heat caused sweat to pool on his brow. Egor acted as support as if he were one column himself, towering strong over Solomon as he shook from the heaviness of the machine reverberations.

Victoria had an overwhelming sense of love that coursed through her body. She loved her sister, Tyler, Abuela, and the elders. It took over the mounting dread.

Love was greater than fear.

Betty Lou kissed Solomon on the cheek. "You are my hero, dear. You put those demons out of commission."

Solomon grinned as he ribbed Egor. "She kissed me. By golly, she kissed me."

Egor's face changed as he held out his arms to shield them all. His shaggy eyebrows furrowed together, and his frown deepened. He enveloped them with his embrace and towered over them. This accounted as her first group hug, but it wasn't the meaning behind the gesture. His protective nature took over, and he took the brunt of the shattering glass that started as a fissure crack, then exploded in mighty shrapnel.

Betty Lou cried out. A shard of glass pierced her arm. Blood poured from the cut. Egor released them, picked her up, removed his tie and wrapped it around her arm as a tourniquet.

Solomon said, "It's my fault wanting to show off."

Betty Lou yelled over Egor's massive shoulder. "It was the spawns from hell's fault. Hush up your blaming and let Egor take me to a hospital. This requires more than Dorothy's patch-me-up bag."

"I'm going with you."

"No, you aren't. Listen, Solomon. I'll be fine. They won't if you leave them in the House of Mirrors alone. Clean up this mess, and I'll see you soon, my love."

Solomon kissed Betty Lou one more time and said a prayer before Egor took her away.

Solomon shook. "What made me want to build this room? Guess a childhood love of the old carney traveling shows down at the sandy lot. You ever been to one of those roadside shows and stepped into a carnival house?"

Tyler said, "I went to one at the State Fair, but it was nothing compared to this. You've got one cool imagination, Solomon."

"Well, I guess I've to get creative again. I will tear this whole room out and replace it with something that Betty Lou has wanted for years, and I just couldn't bring myself to do it. It's too creepy."

Victoria said, "Creepier than this? I don't think so."

"Trust me. That crazy woman has always dreamed to put her porcelain and baby doll collection in a showcase room. It even freaks me out talking about it."

"You just sent handfuls of demons back to hell with their pants on fire and you're afraid of dolls with no souls."

He shuddered and mumbled as if not to stir the spirits, "Then, you have a lot to learn about our line of work."

What unnerved Victoria the most was that those monsters, the ones of no flesh and bone, could cross the divide from the depths of purgatory, tormenting and taunting as they desired. How many demons walked around her? Were they snapping at her heels, a stranger on a street corner?

She told them, "Abrianna must be special to these fiends for them to cause so much destruction and send an army against us."

Abuela said, "This goes way deeper than Abrianna. My spirit tells me it's about rooting out the light. Get to Manuel's family and loved ones. Wipe out the leaders of the ASPs in the process and have nothing standing in their way to carry out their death penalty on unknowing Earthly souls."

Tyler said, "Let's give these devils life without parole and send them back to their prison of hell."

Solomon stopped and pointed. "More around the next turn. No flames this time. I heated the glass without thinking, and that's why it exploded."

Victoria was unsure how much time passed but she could tell was her mind battled against exhaustion. Waiting for Abrianna's full physical recovery wasn't the best plan. They must take the risk. With the demons cast from the mansion, no more red dots on the screen showing house invasion, how long before new legions arrive to fight? Would it be a barrage of satanic forces against them forever?

As daylight broke through the stained-glass windows of the mansion, Abuela spoke for the first time since going into the House of Mirrors. Her voice shook, "For if anyone is a hearer of the word and not a doer, he is like a man who looks at his natural face in a mirror..."

Father Jacoby's deep voice echoed in the corridor, "For once he has looked at himself and gone away, he has immediately forgotten what kind of person he was."

"Didn't I tell you to stop interrupting my sentences? If anyone in this team far and wide is a show-off, it's Father Jacoby."

He gave her arm a soft squeeze. "Thanks for forgiving me."

"Nothing to forgive. We are family, Jacoby. We make mistakes, we come back together, and we move on."

Egor helped Betty Lou enter the room. Solomon rushed to Betty Lou and kissed her full on the mouth. When he released her, he said, "Now, you don't leave my side, woman. You are mine."

"Forever and a day."

"And the day after that."

Tyler said, "Look, they do it, too."

Abuela said, "That's what lovebirds do, they coo, coo each other all day long."

Dorothy interjected, "It drives me cuckoo!"

Father Jacoby reminded them. "Faith, hope and love, but the greatest of these is love."

"Yeah, I know, I know," answered Dorothy. She reached over to her sister and said, "I will love you forever, never forget that."

Betty Lou answered, "Don't worry, I won't. You remind me every day."

Solomon reassured them as he opened the door to the library. "We have the gushy-mushy stuff taken care of, so let's get to the lab. There's no way the demon found his way inside."

"That's why I've been waiting for you here. I smell him. He is close."

Growls, laced with tones that were more animal and ancient, came from the entity. He stood before them as a full demon, no skin covering or masks to blend into the world's surroundings. His fiery red muscular chest expanded, he had scales for legs, a copperhead tail whipped the furniture, distracting anyone who tried to stare too long at the beast. Two antlered length horns crested its wicked face of fangs and burnt streams of scars. If this were the demon from a child's nightmare, then one would never sleep again.

Victoria held up the crucifix and regardless of how much she recognized his power, she knew that his defeat was imminent. Before she could say her prayers, the demon attacked.

He mocked. "I've seen that cross before from that fool, Manuel. I was there, you know."

Abuela commanded, "Don't you dare speak his name, you wicked spawn of Satan."

"I could have made it quicker for him, but you know that stubborn old man. He had to go out of his way. Could have traded his soul for your son's, Jacoby, like you did. But then, he was selfish, too."

Father Jacoby stepped forward, "Heavenly Father, the Creator of Heaven and Earth has forgiven me. You can't throw anything from my past up in my face I haven't already turned over to the Lord. You will not win today, demon."

Tyler and Father Jacoby took three steps, flicking the holy water from the glass bottles they clasped in their hands. Victoria and Abuela prayed the Lord's prayer in Spanish over the demon.

"You won't save him, you know," he taunted. "He will die from your pathetic exorcism. If you had just let him stay with me, he would have ruled kingdoms. He will still rule. If you cast him out today, he will rise again. There is no stopping the separation of the chaff from the wheat."

Victoria stood her ground. "But there will be a stop to devouring her soul or hurting anyone else in my family. In the name of Jesus Christ, I command you to leave us. Remove yourself from our presence. You will no longer harm any of us again. By the power of the Holy Spirit, I cast you and any demons from here to spend your eternity in hell."

The room exploded with a stream of glass as the great window shattered. They all guarded themselves against the brilliance of the light. A winged demon with a cry of mourning and desolation swooped into the room, hovering over the flaming creature. It picked him up and carried him back through the window.

Solomon said, "What was that?"

Father Jacoby answered, "Princes of darkness. I think we are clear of these fiends to take care of Abrianna. They know they've lost or the winged one would have stayed to take revenge. But don't get too comfortable. I tell you this battle will rage another day."

Victoria fell in Tyler's arms. "One more today. Just one more. The most important one of all."

"I'm here with you, baby," he whispered, "It's almost over."

Father Jacoby said, "Are you ready? Do we need to pray? Do you need to rest? Food?"

"No. We need to finish this." She'd save her sister. There could be no other way. She clutched her grandfather's crucifix and held Tyler's hand.

"Say a verse, give me a word or two. Right now."

"You act as if I can just turn this stuff on and off like a switch," he laughed. But it only took him seconds before he spoke her verse, "You will be victorious, for the Lord your God is the one who goes with you to fight for you against your enemies to give you victory."

Solomon patted her. "What a strong name you've got there, young lady."

Abuela smiled. "I named her, who else knew her purpose?"

Victoria's eyes widened. "You knew since I was born? You hid I'd be an exorcist all this time?"

"It's not that you visited much, and if you did you think I'd sit you on my knee and read you stories of how you would one day defeat the legions of hell. You wouldn't have spent time with me again. Adoria would've called me crazy and blocked me with what little time I had with you."

Dorothy said, "We all have our reasons we keep what we see to ourselves. Sometimes it's better that way."

"Sometimes it's not," whispered Abuela.

Father Jacoby said, "God is with us, so who can be against us? Now, save Adrianna. Let us old people rest because I can't remember the last time I pulled an all-nighter?" He sat on the couch and propped up his legs.

Dorothy Lamar leaned over, "I'll keep you company if you want to give it a try."

"You aren't coming?" asked Tyler.

Father Jacoby ignored Dorothy and said, "No, this work isn't for me. No weakened person can enter that room. If that demon says Sam's name to hurt me, I might just suffocate it, and that would end the chance for you to save Abrianna. I am forgiven, but my anger has not subsided."

Betty Lou agreed. "You have the power of the Holy Spirit resting in you. There will be times when we cannot come in and save you. There will be many roads ahead to travel and have none of us with you. Let today be one of those days. Victoria, go save your sister."

Abuela hugged them both. "We will be out here praying for you, lovebirds," appearing to be dozing off as she spoke.

Dorothy Lamar was already snoring.

Tyler said, "Do we need anything else before we go?"

Victoria murmured, "How about strength to do what we must do?

"The Lord covers us with that. He makes us strong in our weakness through the working of the Holy Spirit or that's what I've read. Let's get this over with. I'm tired and hungry and just want to find a place to nibble on some food, and maybe your neck." He worked to pull the vampire face at her as he pounced in and pecked her on the lips.

Victoria whispered, "We've got this, just remember I need you every hour."

"Every hour of every day."

Drum Beats

The door opened to the laboratory. Solomon patted her on the head like an endearing grandfather and shook Tyler's hand. It was as if they were stepping off onto a grand adventure, like a backpacking tour. Instead, they were walking into the mouth of personal hell for Victoria. Her sister's life was at stake. What lies ahead for her was not a campground or a treatment facility crawling with unnatural beings, or an invisible encampment of demon souls.

Victoria's heart yearned for a simple solution that wouldn't cause any more pain to anyone she loved. A wave of vulnerability washed over her and she didn't wear it well. It could paralyze her or she could take action. Only two ways it could turn out for her. She chose to move.

She passed by the booth that Solomon used for his research. They set all of the recording equipment up and now Victoria understood that it was more than just to catch a supernatural experience for a Sunday night documentary. The voice translator was on, and sound panels jumped with the thoughts of the demon. She wanted to focus more on the laboratory than what she would soon face, but the more she tried to look away, the draw of her Spirit pulled her center. In the middle of the room, the circular shaped cage still stood in position. One devil replaced by a new one.

Abrianna said, "Well, it's about time you got here. I've been expecting you." Her voice did not send shock waves through Victoria anymore.

"Abrianna, can you hear me?"

"Your sister is no more. She didn't want to come back."

After what Victoria experienced it was a lie because she'd been battling over the past six months and would have marks like the others in complete possession. Abri might be hidden, yes, but there. Victoria grew accustomed to the trickery, and the realization hit her that demons were the master of all lies, and Jesus the only truth. It was that simple.

"If I would have known you were the exorcist come to destroy me, I would have killed you in your sleep."

"You should've while you had the chance. Today is not one of those days."

Tyler whispered, "Don't speak to the thing. The monitors aren't looking great, Victoria. Her pulse is fading, see the heart monitor."

He pulled out the holy water and took steps toward the pen. He lifted off the top and Victoria followed him, letting him go first to block her view.

Abrianna looked at Tyler with darkened amusement and scowled, "You nobody! You dare even come near me?"

Tyler stopped his forward progression as some presence grabbed hold of his hand. Victoria watched in horror at the motions of the claw-like fingernails filed on her small, bony hands.

The holy water bottle escaped from Tyler's grip and swung upside down, the contents spilling on the floor in a puddle. Shrill laughter broke through their shock.

"I'm the one who requires you to kneel, and soon you shall bow and do my bidding," chortled the wicked one. Tyler yelped with pain at the contact, and his knees twisted. The devil slung him across the room, crashing into the equipment.

Abrianna turned her full attention to Victoria, the neck cracking sounds popping from side to side. "Next?"

"If you're speaking about yourself, then yes. By the power of Christ, I command you, unclean spirit, leave Abrianna Hartwell."

Victoria watched as she inched her way down to the platform and came to stillness as of death. Was it over? She ran to help Tyler to his feet. The knock looked as if it did no physical damage only shook him.

"That was more like a court foul." He tried to play it off, but Victoria felt his hands tremble. He must have had the same thoughts as her because he walked to the monitors. It didn't take a medical degree to pick up on the erratic heartbeat, the missing thumps in the rise and fall where there should have been one.

Victoria prayed, God, give Abrianna a will to fight back and a hope that can only come from you, Lord.

She turned to Tyler. "If she dies right now in that cage, we lose her soul. She never believed in Christ. We didn't, Tyler. I'm not just fighting for her life, but for time to tell her about Jesus."

"Makes everything a little more serious when you think of the ways to an eternity that promises either peace and no more pain or gnawing and gnashing of teeth."

Victoria knelt down and pushed the long curls and tucked them behind Abrianna's ear. Her delicate features were so fragile, so beautiful still. This would strip her innocence from her, change her in ways that nothing ever could. Victoria would have a lifetime to follow Jesus. She prayed that Abri would, too.

Tyler bent down and placed his palms on the floor.

"What are you doing?"

"Let me try something." Tyler scooped up the holy water and sat down beside Victoria. He placed the sign of the cross on her head. "For added protection," he murmured.

He slid his arms through the bars of the cage, grasping Abri's limp head in his hands. The holy water covered her forehead. It was as if an electrical current had jolted Abrianna's body back to life, the jerk rocked them back.

Victoria whispered, "In Jesus' name, release my sister, you prince of darkness, you demon. I command you to tell me your name."

"My name is greater than him you speak. My name will destroy the Heavens and Earth with fire."

Tyler challenged the demon, no longer afraid and filled with the Holy Spirit, "God exalted Christ to the highest place and gave him the name above every name."

Victoria had an idea to catch it with its boastful pride. She stepped around the soundboard that was still functioning and picked up the portable translation device and turned the volume to mute. The screen captioned the vile cursing of murder, death and destruction of the beast.

She taunted, "Your name has no power or authority here."

Tyler understood what Victoria planned, and he took the portable device from her and propped it up on his knees out of sight of the demon.

He laughed. "You are the nobody. Just like Odysseus called out Nobody to the Cyclops in trickery. You hide behind the name of a helpless little girl. I don't know how old you are, and don't care but in my day, we call that a punk."

Victoria smiled. "That was a good one, Tyler. You were paying attention in Freshman English. I'm impressed."

"It was hard to stay focused. You sat in front of me and your hair kept swishing across my desk, and I'd get the smell of you now and then. The memories."

"What is this? The two of you enjoying yourself as I take your sister to hell with me?"

"Is Nobody talking?" Tyler mimicked, trying to catch the rasping tone in the demon's voice.

"Nobody cares if he does," she joked, working to keep her voice calm in this charade. Inside her hope was mounting.

Tyler said, "Baal. His name is Baal."

"What?" shrieked the demon, pushing itself up and scooting backward from the crate. "What did you do? You cannot discover my name before the coming of the harvest. I must separate the chaff from the wheat and burn it all down. My name is no consequence to you, foolish boy. Shut your face!"

Victoria rose to her feet to loom over the shrunk figure against the bars. "Baal, you deceiver of man through the ages. You beast of wickedness. In the name of Christ, I command you, release my sister. I cast you back to hell, Baal. You will never hurt my family again. Father God, remove any diabolical infestations from our lives with the protection of the Father, Son, and Holy Ghost. Amen."

Silence. The translator flashed no more languages. Abrianna choked, her neck rising as her body arched backward. Her hair, matted and soaking wet, hung down as she clung to the sides of the cage like a beast disoriented. The surge of the black vapor hit like a tidal wave passing across their faces and dissolved.

Tyler murmured, "Get behind me Satan."

Victoria repeated it as she opened the door of the cage with the passcode that Solomon had whispered to her as she left them. Triple threes were easy to recall, the Trinity. Tyler bent down beside her sister and pulled her up as if not to break her.

Abrianna reminded her of a porcelain doll that Betty Lou collected. Her feeble voice murmured, "What happened? Where am I?"

Tears flooded Victoria's cheeks, and she pushed them back with her hands. Thank you, God.

She would remember none of this as it should be. Victoria carried enough for them both. She slid the crucifix in her back pocket and opened the door that led into the study. Heads turned as they entered, and Abuela was the first to greet them.

She kissed Abrianna on the cheek. "Gracias, Dios. Eres mi guardián y salvador. Mi Nieta, mi Nieta."

Abrianna looked to each face huddled around her and said, "I'm hungry."

Tyler laughed. "Finally, someone understands me."

Solomon clapped and spoke to no one in particular, the air. "We deserve a feast prepared."

Tyler cut in, "A taco feast?"

Solomon continued speaking, "Whatever Tyler wants, and call Dr. Ivy. I think we all need a good checking out." He pressed his hands against Abrianna's cheeks. "Abrianna needs to be under direct care for the next few days, but we can do that here with our people. Keeping this quiet is the only way."

Victoria thought, our people. My people. She was humbled to be part of God's plan for those He had chosen across the ages to battle against the forces of darkness and together and they could overcome any evil that tried to rise against them. How could she thank them for what they sacrificed and endured to save her sister? Egor and Dorothy entered just as Tyler was lowering Abrianna's feeble body to the couch.

Dorothy took a beautiful butterfly chest from around her back. "Took a little detour on the way back from getting all bandaged up." She handed it to Victoria. "Egor picked it out."

It was such a delicate design and at the contrast of Egor standing, his grin sheepish, spreading across his face in the bulkiest of frames she had ever been close to, endeared him to her. Victoria opened the lid of the box and took out a Bible verse journal and pen.

Abuela said, "Now you can document your first deliverance."

She remembered the style of her Abuelo and flipped to the first page. Would she count all of the demons that came before her, beginning with the camp? Would she list the demonic forces that attacked them at the treatment center or even Father Jacoby's release from bondage? She knew it wasn't the right thing to do and prayed where to start.

June 28 – the exorcism of the child was successful. Age 13, in God's show of ultimate grace and mercy He made her whole again, with no recollection of the attacks. Instructions to a sibling – cleanse the home, witness to the family, bring them into the faith to follow The Way, baptize any left members. Duration: Six months. The name was Baal.

She closed the book and put it back into the ornate box. Would it be her first and last entry, or would she spend a lifetime collecting journals? Only time would tell. Only God would know.

Victoria was sure of one part. No matter what she'd face, she wouldn't be alone. Her two-by-two sat beside her and brought her hands up to kiss them.

She said, "Say something, a verse, anything."

Emotion packed his eyes to a glistening brown. "God is within her, she will not fail."

Victoria cupped his face in her hands and leaned in to nose touching. She felt his breath against her lips, and she leaned in for a deep kiss. She whispered against his lips. "I need you every hour."

"Every hour of every day."

"You think we might get to visit my Papi now? I haven't heard anything from Mami, and knowing her, she's drowning in that hospital alone. I know it's crazy to think of life getting back to normal after all of this. Like writing songs or going on a first date."

"Who needs normal? It's overrated. I've got an exorcist as a girlfriend. I think I've got the rest of my life to get used to this two-by-two gig. Hey, maybe that's what we can call our band?"

She put her fingers through his belt loops. "Always coming up with a plan, aren't you?"

"As long as you are in it, I'm good." He put his arms around her and pulled her close.

Her head rested against his chest and she felt the strong and steady beat like a fist to a hand drum. She knew his heart beat now for her. The embrace let her know just how much it did.

Epilogue

Epilogue

The thud, thud, thud of the boat beating against the pier landing beams beckoned Adoria to walk closer. She pulled at the rope, untwisting it from the double-crossed line, curling around her wrist, pulling it towards her body with all her might. With a snap of wind, she felt as if an unseen force, an angel in that last tug of freedom helped her.

She stepped into the boat, steadying herself as the rocking intensified. The lake appeared to be peaceful from the embankment seemed to be teeming and swirling under the depths with something volatile. Negative.

With a trajectory of its own, the boat moved her to the middle of the lake. There was no motor, no oars. No lifeline or jackets. Somewhere her mind told her she'd forgotten that she didn't know how to swim. That didn't matter now as the monster lurking and calling to her from the bottom of the lake bid her to come.

Adoria leaned over and caught her distorted and ugly reflection in the water. She always knew she wasn't much to look at, but what she saw today spoke volumes of how hideous she'd become. She heard it once more as she held onto the rope as if it were something, anything connecting her to another object, another being.

Adoria could not resist the calling. The sound was morbid yet soothing, a comfort to a soul on fire. She leaned over the edge and sank below the surface, holding onto the rope as the boat capsized above her.

Trailing, trailing, further down.

Down below the lake.

Thanks for Reading

I would love it if you could add a review online at Amazon or Barnes & Noble! Reviews really help an author and thank you in advance for supporting my work!

I would love to see your photos with the book! Please share social media reviews, and challenge others to pick up the series. Don't forget to tag me @jenlowrywrites so that I can join in on spreading the love around!

Happy Reading Book Two of The Hartwell Chronicles Teenage Exorcist (December 13, 2019)

Don't forget to sign up for my monthly newsletter at www.jenlowrywrties.com to catch the latest author news, contests, and more!

Patreon Behind the Scenes Author Life, Pajama Hangouts, Author Gift Boxes, and More at

https://www.patreon.com/JenLowry

Acknowledgements

There are so many people I could thank who have supported me while writing this book. I'm so blessed to have such an encouraging and praying group of family, friends, and coworkers. To my hometown people of Maxton and Robeson County, I miss all of you dearly. There's no place like home, I guarantee that. You've left a permanent marking on my heart, and I hope I've represented you well in this series. You guys are the best.

Lord, I bet my family is happy this book is published and away from my computer screen because I'm sure they heard enough about it. From brainstorming to edits, you guys put up with me. All I can think of to say back is I love you.

To all of my teachers that inspired me! To my 5th-grade teacher, Mrs. Joan Carol Locklear, (I hope you don't mind Tyler having your last name). You read Jack Tales to us in the afternoons before the bell, and I'll never forget your loving smile and kindness!

To Mrs. Brownie Wethington (Jacoby had to have your name!), my 6th - 8th ELA teacher. What a blessing it was for me to have you for three years. For all of our talks during recess at the park bench by the road, for supporting my writing dreams, and for instilling in me a love of literature. My momma bought me that typewriter at the end of my 8th-grade year because I was steady writing down stories and poems in notebooks!

To Mrs. Helen Barrington for having us rewrite Romeo & Juliet in 9th grade. You all know I made it a happy ending. Thank you for all of those trips to your home, for making homemade bread, and teaching me what a tea cozy is.

To my senior English teacher, Mrs. Frances Altman, for having the warmest, most inviting classroom I'd ever been in. For letting Daddy come in and share his Vietnam stories. For making us write that autobiography, that my daddy ended up writing secretly on his own and leaving behind for us to find after he passed away. All of you have made a tremendous impact on my life, and I thank you.

To every student I've had the honor of teaching. You are all my babies forever.

Boys, I hope you see your momma chasing her dreams. Go after yours, whatever they may be. Know I will be here for you every step of the way. You know this book is for my grandchildren (ONE DAY - after you graduate from college and get married to a wife I choose). They will pick up this book and have a Lumbee Indian character, and they can see themselves in the story. My Puerto Rican grandbabies will have Victoria to look up to, and I'll be their Abuela one day, hopefully in a paranormal group being a prayer warrior by then! Okay, I cried at that one. Let me move on...

To all of my readers that have stepped into The Hartwell Chronicles: Teenage Exorcist world – welcome. I'm so glad you're here.

Author Bio

Jen Lowry lives outside of Raleigh, North Carolina and is a proud native of Robeson County. She is the author of a YA contemporary fiction novel, Sweet Potato Jones (2020 with Swoon Romance) and the best-selling Everyday Mom Challenge series. You'll find her enjoying every second of life spent with her family (preferably in pajamas). If you ask her what she's reading it's probably more than one book. Learn more about Jen at www.jenlowrywrites.com and follow her online @jenlowrywrites.

Author's Note

If you, a friend, or a loved one needs help, please don't keep it inside.

There are family, guidance counselors, teachers, community and nationwide organizations that can offer help.

National Alliance on Mental Illness (NAMI): https://www.nami.org/
1-800-950-6264
TEXT NAMI to 741741

National Suicide Prevention Hotline:
https://suicidepreventionlifeline.org/
1-800-273-8255
TEXT HOME to 741741

Atrium Health Call Center
1-704-444-2400

Mental Health Resources http://www.mhresources.org

American Psychology Association http://www.psychiatry.org/mental-health/